Glacier HIGHWAY

DONNA V BATT

LifeRich
PUBLISHING

This is a work of fiction. All of the characters, names, incidents, organizations, and dialogue in this novel are either the products of the author's imagination or are used fictitiously.

LifeRich Publishing is a registered trademark of
The Reader's Digest Association, Inc.

LifeRich Publishing books may be ordered through booksellers or by contacting:

LifeRich Publishing
1663 Liberty Drive
Bloomington, IN 47403
www.liferichpublishing.com
844-686-9607

ISBN: 978-1-4897-3983-4 (sc)
ISBN: 978-1-4897-3982-7 (hc)
ISBN: 978-1-4897-3984-1 (e)

Library of Congress Control Number: 2021925757

Print information available on the last page.

LifeRich Publishing rev. date: 12/24/2021

To the King of kings. I am His daughter and am so thankful for His love and grace.

And to my BFF, Kim Buber. She is my Barnabas. She has encouraged me and walked with me, and she read the book more than once and gave invaluable feedback. She is one of my most treasured gifts.

CONTENTS

AUTHOR'S NOTE

My mother instilled in me the desire to read. I have had so many adventures in my life, and many of them have been through books.

When I began to think about retirement and what to do, I felt the Lord led me to put down on paper the stories I had begun in my mind. This has been quite an adventure. I am so thankful for the family and friends who have encouraged me along the way. Special thanks to D'Amigas. You are awesome.

My hope and prayer for this book is that it might bring joy to some. I pray my witness might help at least one person see the wonder of being a child of God.

Enjoy!

CHAPTER 1

Jen

Jen watched, her dog, CD, go into the brush following a new scent. She smiled, looked up, and felt the sun on her face. She closed her eyes and took in the smell of the evergreens and fresh air. The smell of mildew and decay would come later in the summer. For now, it was just fresh air. It was a good day. Spring in the mountains was her favorite time of the year. She sent up a quick prayer of thanks. She was home and safe. A day in the mountains was a treat.

Jen and CD had spent the last two hours hiking near Avalanche Campground at the base of Glacier Park. There was still a lot of snow, and she had to walk over several piles of still-melting snow and mud. The Going-to-the-Sun Road would not be open for several months, even with the early spring. She remembered when her father and grandmother, Nana, would bring her to Avalanche Campground on Mother's Day. They would bring a picnic lunch, hike, and throw a Frisbee. Occasionally, they would hear the rumble. The warmer weather would begin the spring thaw, and as the snow melted, sheets of it would begin to break apart and create an avalanche. The rumble was the sound of the snow moving, and if they looked up at the right time, they could see the snow cascade down the mountain. She missed her grandmother, but the memories brought a smile. It had been such a good time, a safe time for her.

She was glad she had decided to wear a jacket and her hiking boots. The trails had not been cleared yet, so the walking was a little more difficult than usual. She had not planned to be out long, but CD was having such a good time they had just kept hiking. A wind had come up, and it was a little chilly. She reached down and massaged her thigh; it hadn't been that long since she had gotten out of the hospital. It still ached when she walked too much.

She heard a rumble and looked up to see the snow going over the side of a mountain. She had come on a good day. She always got a thrill when she saw the snow avalanching. She was almost back to the parking lot when she rounded the bend and saw two scruffy men coming toward her. One was tall and dirty with a leering grin. The other was shorter with the same look. She took a deep breath. She remembered seeing them in the old van that had been parked at the service station where she had stopped to get gas and water. They didn't seem to be the hiking type.

"Hey, pretty lady, what do you say you come with us, and we'll have a little picnic."

Jen shook her head and started to move past them down the trail. The tallest grabbed her arm, and she brushed him away.

"Come on. Don't be that way. It—" That's all he got out before she knocked him to the ground with one move. Just as she did that, the other grabbed her. She kicked him in the knee, and he went down, but her foot slipped on the patch of snow, and she started to fall. As she caught herself, the first one grabbed her legs and pulled her to the ground. She struggled, kicking and screaming. She got up and felt something hit her in the back of the leg where she had been shot a year ago. As she went down again, she whispered a prayer, "Please, God, help." They started dragging her down the trail. She continued fighting, but their grip was tight. She saw one pull something out of his pocket that looked like a needle. The last thing she saw was fur flying.

Suddenly she was surrounded by gunfire. She saw Rog hit and heard CD yelp. She felt the pain in her leg. It seemed to last for hours.

The fog started clearing, and she heard screaming. "Call him off, call him off!"

She looked up and saw CD had one man down with his mouth wrapped around his throat. She saw the other one standing with his hands up, looking behind her. She heard an insistent voice saying, "Ma'am, are you OK? Are you hurt?"

She looked behind her to where the voice was coming from and saw a tall man with a gun extended from his hand. "Are you OK?"

Jen nodded, waited a few beats, then said, "Release, CD."

Jen started to get up and felt her leg start to give way. The man with the gun put out one hand and helped her up. When his hand touched hers, she felt a jolt, sort of like when you walk across a rug and touch something; it snaps with electricity.

"I'm Agent Zack Julion, Homeland Security. Are you OK, ma'am?" She nodded as she saw him take out handcuffs and plastic ties for her attackers. She noticed the one that CD had attacked had wet himself in fear. She tried to hide a little smile. She thought he could now say he had the pee scared out of him.

"Did they hurt you?" Agent Julion asked.

"I'm … I'm fine. Glad you came along when you did. Although CD had it under control." She smiled.

"I'm taking these two in. Would you be willing to come down to the station and give a statement?"

She nodded. CD came and rubbed against her leg. She patted his head. "Good job, CD."

They walked toward the parking lot, the two men in front of them. CD walked closely next to her. She told him she had seen the two men at the service station when she stopped there.

As they walked, he shared with her that he had recently been assigned to the Whitefish area. He had grown up in Hamilton, sixty-nine miles south of Missoula, and wanted to get back to Montana after he left the Rangers.

As they walked, she snuck glances at him. He was tall, probably 6'2" at least. He had on a jacket but appeared to be fit. His hair was dark and fairly short, but maybe he needed a haircut because it was a little unruly. Some of the hair fell across his forehead. He smelled of outdoors and had an easy smile. She found him very nice to look at.

He asked about CD, and she told him that he was a retired military dog. He started to ask more questions but picked up on the tension in her body and let it go.

Just as they neared the bottom of the trail, the two men took off running. "You've got to be kidding," Agent Julion mumbled as he went after them. In a few strides, he had knocked the first one to the ground, but the other one was ahead of him.

Jen smiled. "CD, takedown." The dog took off running and then jumped on the back of the one getting away, knocking him down.

"Stop, stop, I give up."

"CD, release." The dog backed away but stood guard.

Agent Julion walked over and hauled the man to his feet. Jen noticed he wasn't breathing hard; he must be in good shape. She shook her head. Why would she even notice that?

"Thanks, CD. I may need to deputize you."

Jen looked at him. puzzled.

"The dog." He grinned.

"Deputy Charlie David Dog. It has a nice ring to it." She smiled.

He pushed the man toward the other one. "Now move. Let's see, resisting arrest can be added to the charges. Want to add any more?" Both men shook their heads and moved forward. Agent Julion pointed them toward a black SUV, opened the back door, and put them in.

"Do you know where the office is? Are you OK with coming in now?"

"I'm not sure. Is it at the police station?"

Agent Julion affirmed it was at the police station. He walked her to her car, a red Toyota RAV. She got in and pushed the button to open the back door for CD. Agent Julion came around to her door. "Are you feeling OK to drive?"

She assured him she was, and then eyed her muddy clothes. "CD is wet, so I think I'll drop him by my house on the way and take time to change if you're OK with that. Then I'll come over. It will just take a few minutes."

He turned to look at her. "No problem. I'll see you soon."

Jen started a little. She had not looked him directly in the face before. He had startling blue eyes, and the smile—*well*, the smile. She nodded.

As she drove home, she shook herself. She wasn't sure why she was noticing so much about Agent Julion, but she needed to get it under control.

When she arrived at the police station, Agent Julion had already taken the offenders to the jail, and they were being booked. He took her into an interview room and talked with her and had her write out her statement. She felt frustrated because she could not tell him anything that would help. When she got up to say goodbye and thank him, he shook her hand and held it for a few extra seconds. "I hope I see you around." He gave her a full smile, and the blue eyes twinkled.

"Uh, me too. And thanks for helping me."

On the short drive home, she kept seeing that smile and those eyes. The only word that came to mind was *nice*.

CHAPTER 2

Zack

Zack nodded at the barista as she brought him his coffee. His lips twisted into a slight smile as he thought of what his fellow Rangers would think if they saw him drinking this "girlie drink." He would never live it down. The Coffee Hut had the best coffee he had ever had, and the mocha gave him his daily chocolate, so it was all good.

On shelves near the ceiling was an arrangement of coffee pots of every size and every kind. It was like getting a history lesson in coffee pots. The display cases were lined with tempting pastries and salads. Tables of various sizes were scattered about.

He stepped outside to where three small tables and chairs were arranged. It was too nice to sit inside even if it was a little chilly. He stretched out his legs and smelled the fresh air and coffee. He closed his eyes. His thoughts drifted to the day before and the smell of the woman in the park. Jen smelled like fresh air and cherry blossoms. When he saw the two men grab her, he wasn't sure he would get to her in time. Her dog had flown out of the bushes at the one man, and it seemed like a movie. He had drawn his gun and warned the men not to move. She seemed out of it, confused, and like she was not sure where she was. When he had first asked if she was OK, she seemed startled, and he had to ask several times before she appeared to hear him and answer.

They had talked on the way down the trail, but he had trouble concentrating. She was about 5'4" and had beautiful, curly, light brown hair. He had been surprised when he saw her eyes, not quite blue but not quite green; her driver's license said *hazel*. She had been limping. He had wanted to ask about it, but her reserve put off the vibe that she did not want to talk about herself.

When he opened his eyes, the woman of his thoughts was standing in front of him. She was dressed in a red top, a black jacket, and black pants that fit her very nicely. His eyes were drawn to the cross necklace she had on. He took a deep breath.

"Well, Agent Julion, fancy meeting you here." The smile reached her eyes.

"Call me Zack," he said. "Could I buy you some coffee?"

She nodded at her hand that held a coffee cup. "No but thanks."

"Have a seat?"

She nodded and sat down. "Sit," she commanded her dog, and he immediately obeyed.

"I noticed you are wearing a necklace, a cross."

She turned her surprised eyes on him. "Well, after yesterday, I was reminded how quickly things can happen, and God helped me through another dangerous time. I wanted to be reminded of it every time I look in the mirror or touch my neck—that God got me through it, and I am safe. Are you a believer, Agent Julion?"

He nodded. "Yes, and I am thankful every day for the gift of salvation I have been given." She smiled. He noticed her smile reached her eyes. Some people smiled but only with their lips; hers was with her whole face. CD stood up and seemed restless.

"Tell me about your dog, CD."

"He is a retired military dog. We served together. We both got injured, so they retired us at the same time. His name is actually Charlie David, but CD is just easier."

"How long ago did you get out?'

"I was injured about a year ago, and after six months in the hospital and rehab, I was discharged."

"Was he your dog?"

She shook her head and looked sad. "His handler was my best friend, but I hung with Rog and CD all the time." Then she seemed to withdraw and get a haunted look. "On our last mission, things went wrong. Rog got killed, and CD and I got injured."

"I'm so sorry. It must be difficult. I was a Ranger. Just got out about a year ago and became a Homeland Security agent. Sometimes it's difficult to adjust to civilian life."

She nodded.

A scream pierced the air. CD raced toward the street and jumped on a man who held the arm of a young woman. The man knocked CD away. A car was idling next to him. He quickly got into the car, and it raced away.

Zack and Jen reached the woman at the same time. CD stood guard. The woman was crying and rubbing her arms.

Zack grabbed a chair from an outside table of the Coffee Hut and helped the woman sit down. Zack asked if she was OK and what happened.

The woman continued to cry. In between sobs, she explained that she had been kidnapped several days ago, and two men were taking her somewhere; she did not know where. They were going through town and had slowed down so someone could walk across the street. She was able to get her door unlocked and jumped out. The man had bolted from the car and grabbed her, and that was when CD attacked him.

Zack told her that he was an agent for Homeland Security, and he would like to take her in and get her statement. He would also help her get in touch with her family. He looked at Jen, nodded, and led the woman toward his car.

He was angry and focused. He could hardly believe this had happened today, but it might give him some leads to what he was there for. He said a quick prayer of thanksgiving for the rescue of the woman. He asked for guidance in the days ahead.

CHAPTER 3

Jen

After leaving Agent Julion and the woman, Jen walked toward her office in deep thought. What had that been about? Why would someone kidnap a woman? She had heard there was a lot of human trafficking but had never given it much thought. Could this be something like that?

She pulled out her key and unlocked the door. *Mountain Rentals* it read on the door. She stepped into the office. It was a large room with two cherrywood desks, with a phone and computer screen resting on top of each. To the side was a waiting area with a white leather couch and love seat, a maroon high-backed chair, and a coffee table with magazines on it. The front of the office faced the street. There were three large windows to look out.

Jen's Nana had owned the business. Jen inherited it when she died almost two years ago. It was a long- and short-term rental place for properties. Some were residential, and some were for short-term vacation rentals. It had been sad to come home with Nana not there, but she was thankful for the business her grandmother had left her. When she first heard that she had inherited it, she hired an office manager, who ran it while she was gone. When Jen got back into town, she looked over the books and the business and found out the manager had been doing a little skimming, so she fired her. Jen decided to go ahead and run the office for now until she decided what she wanted to do, and then she could look for another manager. In the meantime, it gave her an income and something to do and afforded her flexible hours.

She sat down at the desk and listened to her recorded messages as she powered on her computer. She returned calls and emails and arranged for repairs on a couple of rentals. Only once did her mind drift back to Agent Z.

She went to her computer and started looking at more information about human trafficking. She was surprised to learn that an estimated twenty to forty million people were victims of modern-day slavery. Women and girls made up 71 percent of those, and 29 percent were men and boys. There was an estimated $150 billion profit each year. Another $99 billion in profits were estimated for commercial sexual exploitation. It was estimated that fifty thousand people were brought into the US each year, mostly from Mexico and the Philippines. Others were sold to people outside of the United States.

It appeared the women and children were snatched and transported in small groups to various distribution centers. Some were auctioned off; others were snatched because a particular buyer had requested a certain type. Most often, they were controlled by drugs and fear.

Jen shivered. She could not even begin to imagine how terrible it must be for the victims. She pulled up one of the names of the agencies that were working with victims that had been recovered and sent a hundred-dollar gift. She knew that wasn't enough to do much good, but it was a start.

Jen sent up a prayer for the victims and asked God to show her ways that she could effectively help them.

Jen worked the remainder of the day on contracts and billing. It took her only about one day a week to do most of the office work. She decided it was time to go home. She shut down her computer and turned on the answering machine. When she stood, CD jumped up, eager to leave.

Jen's home was an old two-story house. It sat in the middle of an acre of land. The front had a large driveway and then grass with various flowerbeds around the perimeter. The backyard was large and backed up to a grove of trees.

Jen walked around the car and let CD out. As she walked toward the house, she noticed that the crocus and jonquils were starting to bloom. Spring had officially arrived. She was looking forward to going out in the yard and getting the flowerbeds ready to plant more flowers.

Jen loved gardening. There was something satisfying about digging in the dirt, planting flowers, and pulling weeds. She did some of her best thinking while gardening. She was planning to create a rock garden with a birdbath in the middle at the edge of her back patio. She sighed, wishing it was the weekend so she could get started.

CHAPTER 4

Cara

"You are stupid and worthless."

Cara felt the slap on the face. She tried not to show emotion; it only made it worse. She bent down and began picking up pieces of the broken dishes. She had been going into the dining room to set the table when Mrs. Jensen came around the corner too fast and knocked the dishes from her hand.

When she cleaned up the dishes, she cut herself and started bleeding. Mrs. Jenson hit her again, yelled threats, and told her she was getting blood all over everything. Cara was able to stop the flow of blood with a paper towel. She set the table with other dishes. After the family ate, she was allowed leftovers and then had to clean the kitchen. Next, she would be locked into the small room where there was only a bed, a few meager belongings, and three uniforms. Two were daily uniforms, and the other she was to wear for special occasions, when someone else was in the home. She had no pictures on the walls or any personal items.

Cara lay down on her bed. As much as she disliked the days, with Mrs. Jensen yelling at her and the children poking her and hitting her, she disliked the nights even more. She never knew when he was going to come to her. He did not seem to come as often as he used to; for the first year, it was at least three times a week. The next year, it had been less, but the last few months, it had only been once a week. That was a relief. She had heard them arguing. He had said she was getting too old, that they needed to get someone younger. Mrs. Jenson had argued that he needed to be happy with what he had—and what were they going to do with Cara if he got someone new?

Cara closed her eyes and drifted back to the days before she had been picked up on the street on her way home from school. She had been thrown into the van. They put something over her mouth, and she remembered nothing more until she woke. A week later, she was sold to the Jensons.

Cara thought of her family and her life back home. She liked going to church with her family.

"God, are you there?" She wanted to believe in Him. She still hummed songs she had learned in Sunday school. She remembered how the teacher had told them about how much Jesus loved them. She remembered one story about Joseph. His older brothers had hated him and one day sold him to some men traveling by. Joseph believed in God and prayed to Him. He spent many years in jail and then helped some important man when he interpreted a dream. Then he became an important man and ended up saving a lot of people from starving. His brothers had come to ask for help and did not recognize him, and Joseph helped them. Joseph had told his brothers, "What you used as evil, God used as good."

"God, are you going to use me for good? Do you have plans for me? God, please, are you there?" She drifted off to sleep.

When she woke, she was thankful that the man had not come last night. She put on her uniform and went to serve the family breakfast. Everyone was in a hurry to get somewhere—school, work, shopping. She heard the door lock and the code put in and beep as the last one left. When she first came, she had tried to escape several times. Each time, it ended with severe punishment. After the third try, they put in a security system that they could lock from the outside and then could only be opened from the outside.

She hummed the long-ago Bible songs as she worked. After she had completed all her tasks, she went to her room. The rest of the day, she spent on the cot, waiting for the family to come home.

CHAPTER 5

Zack

Zack had not slept well, so he decided to go to the office early. He was feeling frustrated. The young woman, Teri, had been able to give him little information about the people who had kidnapped her or where she had been taken. She had been snatched when she got off the bus after work. She thought she recognized a man from the neighborhood, and when he approached, he had asked her directions. The man grabbed her and tossed her into a van, and then she felt something on her face, and there was a terrible smell. She woke up later in a room with three other women. One had told her she had been dating that man, and he convinced her they should take a trip together. She said they had been drinking and took some drugs, and then he introduced her to another man who gave her some drugs, and when she woke, she was in the room where Teri had been taken.

The other girl had told Teri a similar story. As they compared notes, they found out each of them were estranged from their families, so no one would look for them. Teri noticed that they had similar looks: blonde hair, blue eyes, just over five feet tall, and slender builds. They had come in and taken pictures, and she overheard one of them comment on taking bets on which one the buyer would choose.

They had been given a shot and put into a van. Teri felt herself get tired and could not keep her eyes open. She woke to yelling, but she did not open her eyes. Apparently, the van had broken down. The two men were fighting about what to do. It seemed the van could not be driven. One man said it was not safe to transport them in a car. The other argued that they needed to get them to the buyer, so they would have to use a car. A third man showed up with a car, and they put the girls in the back seat. One man stayed behind with the van.

She was in that car when they had driven into town and she realized her door could be unlocked. She unlocked it, and when they slowed down for a pedestrian, she made her move and jumped out. One man jumped out and grabbed her, but that was when CD went after him, and the man got back into the car, and they sped away.

Teri had not been able to give much of a description of the men. The girls had been drugged most of the time, and she had been so afraid she kept her head down. One of the girls had confronted one of the men, and he beat her up, careful not to hit her face. He later joked he wanted to make sure he got full price for her, and her pretty face needed to stay pretty.

Zack sighed in frustration. He had run the license plate, but it came up stolen. He had shown her the picture of the two men who had attacked Jen. She had not recognized them. He had questioned the two men for four hours, and they had not revealed any association to a human trafficking ring. He got the impression that they had heard that someone paid for women, and they thought they might make some easy cash. He had hopes that when they were arraigned and realized they would probably spend some jail time, it might encourage them to give him some information about who they had heard would buy women.

His frustration had grown since coming to Montana. He had come to Whitefish to be close to his family but also because it was said to be one of the main highways of human trafficking. The victims would be brought through Whitefish and easily transported to Canada and then to whatever their destination was. The last agent had little luck finding out anything, and when he transferred out to go back to the city, Zack took his place.

A few months before Zack left for boot camp, his best friend had been kidnapped. She was missing three weeks before they found her body. The authorities who had been assigned the case said it looked like she had been held for a while because she had ligature marks on her wrists. They believed she had gotten caught in human trafficking; something had gone wrong, and they shot her. During his time as a Ranger, he believed that he fought for his country and the people he loved and the assurance they would remain free. When he returned home, he wanted to make a difference. This opportunity had presented itself, and he had taken it.

He read over his report and called his supervisor, John. They discussed Jen's almost abduction and Teri's story. They discussed some strategies. His supervisor promised him some time with the analysts to do a search of similar kidnappings.

Zack was feeling edgy. His office was small, about the size of a walk-in closet, with a desk and two chairs. He didn't spend much time in it, but when he did, he started feeling claustrophobic. Sometimes he would go work in the conference room when it was free, just to have more space.

It was definitely time to get out for a while. He decided to go grab coffee and maybe a sandwich. He set out for his destination, the Coffee Hut. His steps seemed to lighten. Maybe he would see Jen and have coffee with her. In fact, he walked over to her office, popped his head in, and asked if she could go get coffee. She was waiting for a phone call and for someone to drop something off. He offered to bring her something back.

She smiled. "Coffee and some of their chicken salad would be heaven."

He nodded and walked toward the Coffee Hut. He found himself whistling as he went.

CHAPTER 6

Jen

Jen woke with a start. It was almost seven. It had been after 2:00 a.m. when she had fallen asleep, and her dreams had been filled with kidnappings and feeling of helplessness. She saw CD standing beside the bed, patiently waiting to be let out. She stretched and was tempted to turn over and get a few more minutes. CD whined.

She jumped out of bed, let CD out, and took a quick shower. She used some makeup, not a lot—some eye shadow and foundation. Today she decided to spray on a little cologne, just in case she came across Agent Z, which was what she was calling him.

Jen's senses were immediately assaulted with the smell of coffee and cinnamon rolls when she walked into the Coffee Hut. Her mouth watered. She ordered a cinnamon roll and her usual mocha and scanned the room. She saw Agent Julion.

She and CD walked over to where he was sitting. He offered her a chair, and she sat down. Deb, the barista, would bring her coffee over to her. Jen was surprised to see CD go up to him and greet him. Agent Z reached down stroked CD's head between his ears. He looked tired.

"He doesn't usually warm up to people. He was trained not to, but you seem to be an exception. How did it go with the woman?" she questioned. "Did the license plate turn anything up? Did you find out who they are? Did you catch them?"

"She is doing OK; she was glad to be safe."

"Human trafficking?"

He looked startled that she would guess that. "I can't comment on an ongoing investigation." He smiled apologetically.

"Well, it was pretty obvious from what little I heard. I hope you catch them. I can't imagine how awful it must be. That was one fear I had to fight in Afghanistan, the fear of being captured."

Deb delivered her coffee, and Jen got up to go. "Good to see you again, Agent Julion."

"Zack, please."

She nodded and left. She felt his eyes on her as she crossed the room. She turned and smiled as she opened the door and left.

CHAPTER 7

Zack

Zack had been impressed that Jen had guessed the human trafficking with such little information. It would have been nice to talk with her and get some input from her. There were advantages to working in a one-person office, but sometimes it would be nice to have a partner to bounce thoughts and ideas with. He had a great supervisor, and they talked frequently, but a partner would be nice, and one that looked and smelled like Jen, well … even better. He needed to stop thinking about her. He had too much to do and needed to stay focused.

He left a tip on the table and went to his office. His office was sixteen by twenty feet. He had a desk, a computer, and two extra chairs. When he had to interview someone, he usually used a conference room down the hall. He had a picture of his mother and brother on his desk, one that had been taken last time he was home. Otherwise, the office was void of anything personal.

He went over the research the other agent had left and called up some other reports from the Department of Justice. He was working several other smaller cases. He decided to drive around and get a little more feel for the place. He had only been there a week, and he didn't have the lay of the land yet. If this place was indeed part of the main highway for trafficking, he needed to figure out what his next move was.

He had added the name of the two men who had attacked Jen to his report. He had checked them out but had found only minor infractions. Still, he wanted to keep a watch on them; they might be connected to the traffickers.

He spent the next two hours driving around town. Then he drove to Big Fork, a town forty miles south. He went back to the office and did some more paperwork. He requested some additional records from the main office. He found his mind drifting to his meetings with Jen. He realized he would like a chance to get to know her a little better. There was something about her that made him want to seek her out and talk with her more. He wanted to ask her about her time in the army and why she had a haunted look when she mentioned her fear of being captured. He wanted to know what she liked to eat. Maybe he would see if he could find her and ask her out to dinner.

He had been surprised to find where she worked. He wasn't sure what she had done in the military but had gotten the idea it was something to do with investigating because she had so quickly picked up on the human trafficking angle.

He walked to her office, and just as he arrived, she and CD came out the door, and she turned to lock up.

"Done for the day?"

She jumped and turned around. "Oh, sorry. Yep, done with the day."

Zack had noted this morning that she looked tired, and he was surprised to see how she jumped when he spoke to her. The look on her face when she turned to him at first showed fear.

"I was just looking for you. I haven't eaten since the muffin I had this morning, and it is dinnertime, and well, I wondered if you would like to get something to eat with me—that is, um, if you don't have any plans." What was wrong with him? He didn't usually get so nervous asking a woman out, even a beautiful one. He had dated plenty of beautiful women. Tamara had been beautiful, but after a year, he realized beauty was not enough. She was self-focused and selfish. His family was glad when they broke up.

"Oh, yeah, I guess that would be nice."

They opted for pizza. They drove their own cars to the pizza place. Jen left CD in her car. They regaled each other with stories from their childhoods. Zack had been one of those kids who lived in the same place all through growing up. His father had died when he was young, and his mother had raised him and his brother on her own. As he told his stories, it sounded like it had been a fun place to grow up. He and his brother, while mischievous, had been close and helped their mom. It made Jen feel a little sad.

He talked about the time he had been with the Rangers and how close he had been to his Ranger brothers. It appeared many of them continued to be in contact.

When she asked why he had gotten out, he told her he had wanted to be closer to his mother and brother. He said he realized that someday he wanted to be married and raise children, and he felt being a Ranger would not have allowed him to be there for his wife and children. What he didn't tell her was about Tamara.

"I hear your dad was a pretty impressive detective at the police department. Tell me more about him."

CHAPTER 8

Jen's Father

Jen paused. "My father is actually a pretty wonderful, amazing man. When he was young, his father was an alcoholic, and his mother left. He had to raise himself pretty much. His grandmother loved him and tried to be there for him, but his father moved him to Wyoming. He didn't get to come back here to see her very often. He apparently got into a lot of trouble. When he was seventeen, he was arrested, and he had two choices—jail or army. He chose the navy and ended up being a Navy Seal. He told me after three years with the Seals, they got trapped on one of their missions. There were fourteen of them, two teams. Something had gone wrong, and they had not been able to meet at the extraction point. They were surrounded in an area of several buildings and were not sure if help was coming. Dad told me one of the guys from the other team asked if they died there, did they know where they were going? Most of the guys blew him off, but Dad went over near him. Over the next few hours, between eruptions of battle, the man told him about Jesus's love for him and His desire to be the Savior to all men. Dad said he had been in a lot of trouble growing up. He had done some things that haunted him. He told the man that God probably didn't want him. The other soldier told him how God loved him, just where he was, and wanted to save him.

"Through the hours of waiting and wondering if they would be rescued, they were constantly under attack. There had been snipers around them. By the time the sun came up and help arrived, her father had given his life to Jesus. Only five soldiers walked out that morning. The soldier that had shared his faith had died just an hour before. Dad held him in his arms as he was dying, and his last words were, "I'll see you on the other side, brother."

"From that day on, my father lived his faith. He loved his Seal brothers but felt God wanted him to do something different. He didn't think he had enough opportunities to witness when he was with his team. He had shared with each of them, and several had repented and become believers. So, as hard as it was, he chose to leave the Seals and became a military policeman.

"Dad went to Germany, and that is where he met Mom. She had come to Germany, where he was stationed, to teach English in one of the German schools. She seldom went to base to socialize, but this Saturday night, her roommate insisted she come with her to a dance. Dad says he saw her, and his heart stopped beating." Jen smiled. "He went up to her and said she was going to be his wife. They dated for six months and got married. They transferred to Japan for several years. I'm not sure how many places they lived, but it seems they had to move a lot. They wanted lots of children, but Mom couldn't seem to get pregnant. After ten years, Mom became pregnant with me. It was a difficult pregnancy, and after she had me, they told her she could not have any more children. I think Mom was always sad about that. Dad always told her, between her and me, he had his hands plenty full, thank you very much. I think he would have liked more children too, but he never let on to Mom.

"They found people to worship with wherever they were. Dad

would walk up to total strangers and begin telling them about Jesus. And every place we left, people would come up to Dad and thank him for leading them to Jesus.

"Mom was a believer when they met. Their home had been one of loving Jesus and serving him. Dad often said that he wanted his life to count for Jesus, to help others come to Jesus, just like the soldier who had witnessed to him. He had not known the soldier's name; he had joined them only hours before the mission. After years of reaching out, he finally found out his name was William Timbers from Great Falls, Montana. The next time he was stationed in the States, Dad drove five hundred miles to Great Falls and found William's mother. He told her how her son had brought him to Christ. His mother had wept with Dad and thanked him for sharing that with her.

"Dad's life was a witness of God and His love. When I was eight, he led me to faith in Jesus as my Savior. After Mom got sick, I prayed to God to heal her. After her death, I was angry with God. Dad just sat with me. He told me he did not have the answers, but he knew that the day would come when we would die, and he knew Mom would be standing with Jesus with open arms to welcome us home. Through the years, I got over my anger at God, but I still question from time to time why people we love must die.

"Dad also had a deep love for his country. Even though he had been pushed into the military, he believed he had a role in serving and keeping the country he loved safe. He instilled this love and dedication in me, so when I graduated from high school, it just seemed natural that I would join up.

"I thought it was normal to move every few years. I regret that even though I make friends easily, I tend to hold them at arm's length. I think that makes it hurt less when you have to say goodbye.

"It had mostly been good until Mom got sick. She had surgery and then was constantly going to appointments. Dad tried to be with her and go to all her appointments, but I saw him become tired and withdrawn, grieving. It almost seemed like I was losing both of them. Then Mom took a turn for the worst, and the military told Dad he was being transferred again. Dad decided to leave the military so he could take care of Mom the last few months of her life. He also left because he felt I needed him around more and not to be constantly moving. We moved to an apartment in Germany, not far from the base. For the first four months, he stayed home and took care of Mom, but then she died. Two days later, we were packed and ready to move. He brought me to Whitefish to be nearer to his grandmother, my Nana."

Jen realized how long she had been talking. "I'm sorry. That was definitely too much information."

Zack leaned in. "No. I love hearing about you. Please keep going."

Jen nodded. "When I think of that time, I remember so much sadness. I could tell he was trying to not show it, trying to make me feel better, trying to help me settle in with Nana and have a somewhat normal life.

"Not long after we came to Whitefish, Dad started working for the Whitefish Police Department. He started as a patrolman, but with the military police background, he was quickly made detective. He started seeming more like his old self, with a touch of sadness always there.

"Whitefish doesn't have a high crime rate, but occasionally Dad would come home with his cases, and we would talk. He would talk about how facts weren't adding up or how he needed to find more information. One time, after we talked, I got on the internet and did some research. I found I had a knack for following threads of information to gain more. When I took the information to Dad, he was astounded at what I had found out, and with that information, he was able to put it together and make an arrest. After that, we often talked about his cases, and I would do research, and together we would come up with theories. It was our way of connecting, and it seemed that, together, we solved several cases. So, after graduation, I joined up. It didn't take me long to realize I would be good working in intelligence and putting pieces of information together. I was fortunate to have a good mentor, and he helped me get into the special intelligence unit. After I left for the military, Dad met Mary. Eventually they married. A year later, Dad retired. Then they moved to Texas to be near her children. Dad works part-time with the local police."

Jen took a breath. "And there you have it." She was embarrassed. She seldom talked much about herself. She looked at her watch and realized they had been there for almost two hours. "I am so sorry. I went on and on and took up your—"

Zack reached over and grabbed her hand. "Thank you, Jen, for being willing to trust me and share with me. I feel honored that you told me about it. I can tell you're feeling a little uncomfortable now. Please don't. I liked it very much." He reached for the ticket. Jen started to reach for her wallet. "No. I have this. Please. I asked you to dinner."

He paid the bill, and they walked out together. He walked her to her car, then opened her door, said hi to CD, smiled, and left.

CHAPTER 9

Jen

Later as she lay in bed, Jen went back over the conversation. She was surprised she had shared so much and even more surprised that it had seemed comfortable. When she had gotten embarrassed, he had been kind and seemed really interested. Zack was something special. She figured he was probably rather good with his job, particularly questioning people and getting information. After all, that was what he was trained to do.

As she thought about Zack, her thoughts lingered on how nice he smelled. Cinnamon and spice. She wasn't sure why she was so attracted to him, except that he was an exceptionally good listener, very handsome—yes, *very* handsome—and nice on top of all that. She had not considered dating or getting involved with anyone since Henry broke up with her after she had been injured.

She and Henry had met when she went home with Rog on their first leave. Her father had been dating Mary, and she just didn't feel up to going home. Rog had invited her to go home with him so she could meet his girl, Cyndy. Henry had been a classmate of Rog's and was funny and handsome, and they had hit it off. It was natural that they became a couple during the month of leave. They hung out together on the next leave. He had hinted that there was a future for them together. She had been only vaguely aware that he needed to be the center of attention and was impatient if things did not go his way.

After Rog died and Jen got out of the hospital, she went to see Rog's parents, Cyndy, and Henry. Her leg was healing, but she still had a severe limp, and when she got out of the car and walked toward Henry to greet him, she noticed a look of disgust on his face. He tried to mask it. They went to a bar they had frequented before with Rog and Cyndy. She met with several people they had hung around when she and Rog had been home. While they were talking with friends, the waitress dropped some glasses, and Jen hit the floor and had a major flashback. When she finally came back to the present, Henry rushed her out and took her home. He said he would call her the next day, but he didn't—or the next or the next. She said her tearful goodbye to Rog's parents and Cyndy without him contacting her again. Over the next couple of months, she recognized that she had dodged a bullet but still felt hurt and broken. She didn't think she would ever open herself up to anyone. She went to see her father and, by that time, his new wife. She loved seeing her father laughing and smiling. She enjoyed getting to know Mary, but she felt like she needed to be on her own. That was when she returned to Whitefish.

Jen felt herself start to drift off, and the last thought she had was, *But Zack is really nice and very nice to look at.*

CHAPTER 10

Rog

Jen woke several times during the night. Her dreams had been filled with Rog. She wasn't surprised because she had been thinking of him the night before.

She met Rog and CD the first month she was in Afghanistan. When she had first arrived, they had been out on a mission. When they returned, looking dirty and unkept, she practically ran them down when she was walking around a corner. CD had immediately gone into protection stance and growled. She froze, looking from this big, mean-looking German shepherd to this grungy, smiling man. She backed away slowly with her hands up. She heard the man say, "CD, it's OK. Friend." The dog relaxed.

"Thanks. I thought he was going to attack me."

"He was. He thought you might be attacking me."

"Um, is he always that fierce?"

"Only with pretty girls that are attacking me." He put out his hand. "Hi, I'm Rog, Roger. This is CD, Charlie David. We just got back from an intense mission, and we are both tired, hungry, and dirty, so CD reacted a little more defensively than normal. Can I buy you dinner and make up for it?"

"Well, we are at the cafeteria, so I guess dinner would be good, as long as you are buying." She smiled.

"It's a good thing we are at the cafeteria and you are a pretty cheap date, since I don't have any money." Jen raised her eyebrows. "Well, not cheap date, but, well …" She laughed.

After that, they became close friends. Rog had a way of drawing her out and getting her to talk about herself. Through the friendship, she realized she often held herself back from people. She had not let many people get to know her. She realized it came from making friends and then having to move away; she had learned not to get too attached. Rog helped her open up.

They worked together and spent off time together for the next two years. Rog became the big brother she always dreamed of. He treated her like a little sister and was a little too overprotective of her when guys on the base tried to hit on her.

It came time for Rog to decide if he would re-up. He shared that he was thinking about getting out. He had asked Cyndy, his girl back home, to marry him. She had said yes. His father had a security business, and Rog planned to join him. Jen began to wonder about what she wanted. The military had been all she had thought about, what she was used to, but she realized it would be empty without Rog. She missed her father and their talks, but he was with Mary now. Jen longed to have friends. She had a couple of friends back in Whitefish. Maybe she needed to go visit.

She had been mulling over all this in her mind when they prepared for the mission that day. She had not known that it would be the day the decision would be made for her—or that it would be that day she would lose her best friend.

CHAPTER 11

Paulie

"Paulie, I think you made that up just to tease me." Jen laughed. Then she saw the hurt look in Paul's eyes.

"You know I can't lie to you; I always tell the truth."

"I'm sorry, Paulie. I didn't mean for that to hurt you. Come on. Let's clean up the dishes, and I'll let you choose the movie tonight." She tossed him the dish towel and started clearing the table.

Sunday night was their night to hang out. Dinner and a movie at the house. They had been doing this for fifteen years, except when she was in the army. When she returned home, they picked up where they had left off.

They quickly cleaned up the kitchen, loaded the dishwasher, and went in to sit down and watch a movie. Paulie picked *The Return of Skywalker*. Jen shook her head. Paulie was the gentlest man she knew, not a mean bone in his body, so she was always surprised when he chose the action movies.

As they watched, Jen drifted back to her third-grade year when they moved to Whitefish. Until then, her father had been in the military, and they had moved around a lot. Her mother had gotten ill when she was in the second grade. Her father retired so he could help take care of her. A year later, she died, and they moved to Whitefish. Jen had been excited to move closer to Nana and that they would not have to move so often.

The first day of school, she had gotten up and dressed an hour before it was time to leave for school. She was excited to meet new friends and know they might stay around for a while, to maybe have a best friend. She walked into the school on air, which was quickly knocked out of her. Her class was filled with extra bullies; at least that was what she decided when she looked back after graduating. They had taunted her and laughed at her clothes. She had not gotten new clothes since her mother was ill. The clothes were typical for Germany but not so much for the States, and they were a little too tight and short. Her fellow students let her know she didn't fit in.

At lunch, she sat at a table, and it was clear everyone had been warned to leave her alone. Her sandwich tasted like dog food—at least what she thought dog food must taste like. She was ready to get up and run from the room when this small boy sat down next to her. He did not say a word, just sat there and ate his lunch. The next day, he did the same.

On the third day, he said only a few words. "My name is Paulie. I have Asperger's." They finished eating in silence and then got up and went to their class.

Jen didn't know what he meant when he said he had Asperger's. When she got to Nana's after school, she asked Nana what it was. Then she poured out the whole story of what had happened, how some of the kids had made fun of her and how others had avoided her, and then how Paulie joined her for lunch. Nana explained that people with Asperger's are as smart as anyone else, but sometimes they have difficulty fitting in, and they have a way of looking at the world differently. The next day, Nana took her shopping and got her some new clothes that fit and would be appropriate for her school.

Jen and Paulie continued to have lunch together every day. They had been close friends ever since. Jen had made other friends, and some even seemed to learn to like Paulie and understand him, but she never let anyone make fun of him or hurt him, and he remained her friend.

Paulie loved CD, and CD seemed to reciprocate the feeling. He was always excited to see him. They seemed to have a special bond. CD usually sat at Paulie's feet on movie night.

"CD was a hero on Thursday," Jen told him. Was it only a few days ago she met Zack? She continued to tell him how he had saved the woman from the man who had kidnapped her. Paulie asked about why they would kidnap her, and Jen explained that it appeared it was part of a human traffic ring. She told him how people would snatch other people or sometime coerce them to come with them, and then they would sell them to others for various purposes.

When Paulie left, he seemed more thoughtful than usual. His goodbye to CD, however, was as sweet as ever. Paulie lay on his back, CD sat on him, and then they wrestled a little. She never saw CD act that way with anyone else. Paulie didn't even like being touched.

As Paulie left, Jen said a prayer of thanks for him and for his friendship through all the years. She was thankful that his relationship with CD was special and gave both so much joy.

CHAPTER 12

Jen

Jen sat on the couch with her legs tucked under her. She had just completed her daily Bible reading and was trying to decide what she wanted to do with her life. She was feeling discontent. The job was not a challenge, and she found herself feeling bored and useless. She had joined the army because she had wanted to do something to protect her family and help people, to make a difference. For the last several months, she had been focusing on strengthening her leg and adjusting to civilian life.

It had been almost two weeks since Jen had met Zack on the mountain trail. She saw him at the Coffee Hut each morning, and he greeted her warmly, but he was usually leaving when she got there. Sometimes she got the impression he might have been waiting just to see her. She felt butterflies in her stomach at that thought. Was he part of her discontentment?

She gave herself a shake. She needed to decide what she wanted to do with her life; she needed to focus on what God wanted for her life.

She decided to make a list of all the things that she had liked about her work in the military: research, finding details and putting them together like a puzzle, the comradery, and the satisfaction in knowing she could make a difference. Then she listed what she liked about the work now: helping people, able to work independently, being at home with her friends in Whitefish.

Her mind wandered back to the evening before when she had dinner with Teresa. She and Teresa had been friends since junior high. While Jen went into the military, Teresa decided to go the University of Montana in Missoula. She became a teacher and currently taught fourth grade.

Last night, Teresa talked about a little boy she had in her class. When he was in the second grade, his parents had gotten divorced. He should have been learning to read, but his mother had told Teresa that his father had become violent, and the little boy had become fearful. He would often act out in class, especially when it was supposed to be quiet time to read. The teacher from the year before had been an older woman. She had told Teresa she would sit him in the corner and tie his mouth shut with paper towel so he would be quiet. Teresa said she had been spending some extra time with him. He was finally learning that he could read and was getting excited. Jen loved the look of joy and satisfaction as Teresa talked about the boy. Jen wanted to feel that kind of satisfaction in a job.

She mentally shook herself and spent time in prayer, then got ready to meet the day. She hoped she would see Zack.

CHAPTER 13

Trevor

Trevor woke with a start. He was confused and disoriented, and every part of his body hurt. Then he remembered he was at the Shed. He had been there for six months. Last night, he had won the fighting match.

Trevor lay back down on the hard bed. His mind drifted back over the last three years—memories that were fading and he wasn't even sure were real.

What he remembered was a coach from his school had invited him over. The coach had found that Trevor's parents were recently divorced, and his father lived sixty miles away. Trevor's mother worked nights. Trevor had been only twelve years old, but he was home alone most nights. His mother worked only a few blocks away, and he could call her if he needed anything. The coach caught him after school one day and asked if he would like to come over for dinner later. He told Trevor not to tell anyone because some of the other boys would think he was playing favorites, but he knew Trevor could use the company.

Trevor had gone home, finished his homework, and walked to the coach's house. When he got there, the coach had welcomed him enthusiastically, and they had eaten dinner. He remembered sitting down in a big chair—and then nothing. Next thing he knew, he woke up in a room with five other boys. Trevor was twelve years old, and the other boys ranged from eight to thirteen. There were two men who would come in and take them one by one into another room. They had made them take off their clothes, and then someone had taken pictures. Then they were returned to the room. They were all so scared; no one knew how they had gotten there or why they were there.

One of the men came into the room and took one of the boys That boy did not return. Then another was taken. Trevor was the third one. He was forced into a van and saw the two other boys. They tied their hands and feet, and then each of them was given a shot. Trevor woke up what must have been hours later. The other boys were gone. They stopped and opened the back door of the van to let him out. He was stiff from sitting so long. He stumbled out and saw a big house and a big man standing there.

"Welcome to your new home." The man took his hand.

"What are you talking about? I want to go home."

The man shook his head. "Your mom and dad decided they couldn't take care of you, so they sent you to live with me."

Trevor didn't believe him but didn't know what to do. He watched the man shake the van driver's hand, and then the driver got into the van and left.

"I want to call my mom now."

The man just shook his head, grabbed his arm, and led him to the house. Trevor tried to pull away and started to run, but the man knocked him down.

"So, I guess we do this the hard way."

The man dragged him into the house and took him to a room that was like a cell. There were no windows or doors except the one he was pushed through. Trevor tried to pull away, and the man hit him in the stomach and threw him on the floor. "Let's see how resistant you are after a couple days of no food."

Trevor searched the room, trying to find a way out. The door was metal, and the walls were solid. True to the man's word, Trevor did not get any food. Occasionally, someone would set some water inside the door. He started getting lightheaded and was so hungry.

Then the man came in. He had a plate of food in his hand. "Are you ready to cooperate?"

Trevor's stomach grumbled, and he nodded. Before the man would let him eat, he made Trevor sit in a chair, and he put something around his leg. He explained it was a tracker. If Trevor tried to run away, they could track him, and they would bring him back. He promised that two days without food would seem like a vacation compared to what awaited him if he ran.

After he ate, the man took him into his bedroom and made him do terrible things. He wanted to throw up but was fearful that the man might not let him eat again.

The next two and a half years were a nightmare. The man continued to do terrible sexual things to him and forced Trevor to do sexual things to him. Sometimes, he would bring other men to join him. Sometimes he would just bring one man at a time. One man who came in several times took joy in beating Trevor with a belt and then sexually abusing him.

The anger in Trevor built. He had tried to escape three times, and each time he was beaten and went days without food. He knew he would have to plan carefully if he was ever to get away.

Then one night the one man was being particularly brutal. Trevor lost it and beat the man up. By the time his keeper heard the noise and realized something was wrong, Trevor had beaten the man to a point his face was no longer recognizable.

The man hit him over the head and hauled him to his cell. The next day, two men came and got him and brought him here to the Shed.

HAPTER 14

Zack

Zack walked into Pizza Hut and immediately heard Jen laughing. He was surprised that he had recognized it as her laugh. He looked around and saw her with a man about her age. They seemed to have an easy comradery. He felt a little jealous.

Jen looked up, saw him, and waved him over. She introduced her friend as Paulie, who corrected her and said, "Just Paul." They invited Zack to join them, so he sat down. Minutes after he sat down, the pizza arrived, and they insisted that he eat it with them.

They ate pizza, drank a beer, and Paul and Jen told him stories of high school. He found out they had been best friends growing up. Paulie told him about how he and Jen had gotten into her father's beer one night and how her father had discovered them with their heads bowed over the toilet because they were sick. Paul assured him that since then, they only had one beer when they drank.

Almost immediately, Zack had noticed that Paul must have Asperger's. He had a cousin who had it, and he saw similar characteristics. He noticed how he talked clearly and in a certain pattern. He noticed mannerisms like his cousin's. He noted that Paul had a ritual with each bite.

Once Paulie realized that Zack was sort of a policemen and had helped CD rescue the woman, he asked a lot of questions, but Zack had to tell him that he could not comment on an ongoing investigation.

For the next ten minutes, Jen shared some of the information she had found on the internet about human trafficking. She told him about the number of people taken each year and the amount of money involved. She went on to talk about how there appeared to be certain highways that the authorities were convinced the traffickers used.

Paulie told them that after Jen had told him about the woman who had been kidnapped, he had done some research of his own. He found that there was evidence that the highway running through Whitefish to Canada was one of the main ways of transporting victims to Canada.

Zack noticed a man and woman a few tables down seemed to be listening in on the conversation. When they saw him watching, they quickly looked away.

As they stood to leave, Paulie turned to Zack and said, "I guess you are my friend now, so you can call me Paulie." They walked to their cars together, and Paulie got into his car and drove away.

Jen and Zack visited for a few more minutes and then said good night.

CHAPTER 15

Jen

Jen held the door, her arms full of groceries, allowing CD to go into the house first. As she put the groceries down, she felt the hair on the back of her neck rise and saw CD go into high alert. He walked around the kitchen and sat at the end of the counter. That was what he had been trained to do when he discovered electronics when they were in the field. He had not done that since they returned from Afghanistan.

Jen kneeled next to him and looked under the counter. There appeared to be a surveillance bug, a listening device placed under her counter. She moved away and called to CD. When he came to her, she gave the usual words of praise when he did his job.

She moved to her purse and pulled out her gun. She walked around the house to make sure no one was there. What did this mean? What was she going to do?

When she first left the army, she moved to the house where her Nana had lived. Her father signed the house over to her when she decided to stay in Whitefish. She had done some remodeling. She knew there had been threats on her life. She had taken some precautions. She had built a safety room. One way she could enter it was through the bathroom, by moving what appeared to be a towel rack. When she lifted the rack, a small door would open into the room. The other side of the room had a door that entered her family room. From that room, it looked only like a bookcase. She had remodeled the family room around the small, new security room and painted it in a way that created an optical illusion that made the room appear larger. This way, no one would notice there was an eight-by-ten space between the bathroom and the family room.

The doors and walls were reinforced with solid wood. Computer monitors lined the walls. At one end was a small desk where three computers had been installed. There was a chair at the desk and another chair set to the side. One four-door filing cabinet sat next to the desk. On top of the cabinet was a two-by-two-foot safe. Two of the computers were monitoring several sites she felt it important to watch. The third computer monitored the cameras she had installed outside and inside the house. Sensors were set around the perimeter of her house that signaled when someone was near the house. When someone stepped inside the range of the perimeter, she could hear windchimes in the house. If she was outside, the signal sounded like frogs—a sound most people would not even hear or pay attention to. She realized she was probably a little paranoid. She had worked in intelligence and security, and there had been threats on her life, so she had decided to error on the side of caution. Now she was glad she had. She had become lazy and not set the lock on her door before leaving today.

She went into the security room and closed the door. She pulled up the recordings from the day and fast-forwarded to where she saw someone enter her house and place the bug. The person looked to be a male Caucasian, about 5'10" and with a muscular build. He was wearing a hat that hid most of his features. At one point, he looked up, and she could see his face. The shot might have been good enough to run through a database to determine who he was; unfortunately, she no longer had access to that program. She printed out a copy and sent a copy to her phone.

She left the room, grabbed a Coke, and went out onto the patio. Was this related to her time in the military?

Her mind went back to those days when she worked with CD and Rog. CD had been trained to sniff out bombs and electronics, as well as protect and keep his handler safe. Jen had met them when she first got to their base and later was assigned to their intelligence team. When they were stateside, they worked mostly with military police. Much of her work had been done searching for missing arms. When they were deployed, she was typically working at a command center, working with information gathering. She would decipher information gathered from various types of electronic that had been confiscated. Occasionally, she joined the team in the field. That had been the case on their last mission when they were in the field.

Rog and CD worked as a team. They would go into a building, searching for bombs and electronics. Sometimes they would download information from computers they found; other times they would bring back the computers so they could be gone over more thoroughly.

Jen's and Rog's skills had been complementary. They were touted the best in the field. On two occasions when they were stateside, they had discovered some traitors in the ranks and had to work with the authorities to take them down.

On days off, Rog and Jen and CD spent most of their time together. They laughed and played and shared their secrets. Rog told Jen about his plan to ask Cyndy to marry him, and together they had come up with a romantic plan for how to do that. Jen was thrilled for Rog when Cyndy said yes.

Jen had noticed that while CD was excellent at his job ferreting out electronics, he also seemed to have a sixth sense when someone was in trouble. He was protective of anyone he seemed to think might need help or rescuing.

One Saturday, they had gone to a local town and were walking around enjoying some downtime. There was destruction all around them where buildings had been bombed. Buildings were in rubble next to buildings that appeared untouched. Suddenly CD took off. They raced after him. He was making his way down a pile of rubble where a building had been. When they called him to come back, he continued to go down into the rubble. They followed him. They discovered a little girl who had apparently been playing nearby when her ball had rolled into the hole. She tried reaching for it, fell through a floorboard, and was not able to get out. She was crying and yelling for help. They dug their way through some of the debris and pulled her out, just as her mother came frantically running toward her. The little girl had given CD a fierce hug before she left with her mother.

Then, the last mission. They went into a warehouse where there had been some ISIS operatives. They had determined there were no bombs. CD had found some electronics hidden in a "hidey hole," and they were just about to gather it up. Suddenly some of the enemy soldiers burst into the room and started shooting. They hit Rog in the stomach, Jen in the leg, and CD in the back leg.

Friendly troops had responded quickly and taken them out. CD had crawled over to Rog and tried to stand guard. When the medics came in and went to check on Rog, CD almost attacked them before Jen was able to command him to stand down. The last thing she remembered was hearing someone say Rog was dead and hearing CD howl. Then she passed out.

She and Rog had made some enemies when they had investigated their fellow soldiers. They found a group of soldiers who were stealing arms and selling them. Between the two of them, Rog and Jen had gathered enough evidence that they were arrested and court-martialed. Some of their fellow soldiers resented that they had been digging into their personal lives. They made enemies of those who had been arrested. Her commander told her there had been threats made on her life.

"Could this be from one of those people?"

She debated what she could do. If her father was still in the police department, she would have taken it directly to him. Her impression of the current police chief was he was a politician and probably wouldn't help her. She had not met the new sheriff, so she didn't feel comfortable going to him. Could she mention it to Zack and see what he thought?

CHAPTER 16

CD

Charlie David (CD) came from a long line of service dogs. His parents were full-blooded German shepherds. His father weighed more than eighty pounds and was almost all black. His mother was smaller, about sixty pounds, light colored, and medium sized. They made beautiful puppies, and most of them ended up in some type of law enforcement.

CD was large like his father. He weighed eighty-two pounds. Even being that big, he was fast and powerful. He had a beautiful coat of mixed colors. He had his mother's light fur, but it was tipped with black. It looked like someone had taken him to a beauty shop and had put the dark tips on. More than once, women had commented to Jen that they wished they could get their hair color to look like that.

As a puppy, he had been unusually curious. The owners hid toys all over the house, and CD would find them, bring them in, and pile them at his owners' feet. CD also seemed to be protective of everyone in the house. Once a neighbor had come by and was angry about a car being parked too near his driveway. CD stood and went into an alert mode, growling until the neighbor calmed down. Once one of the other puppies from the litter had gotten rough with the four-year-old girl in the house, and CD had nipped his sibling until he backed away.

After being weaned, he was taken to the base and put with other dogs to see if he could be trained. He was matched with a handler. At first the training had gone well, but his handler was unusually rough, and things started going sideways when he hit CD after an exercise. CD turned to nip him. The handler wanted him taken out of the program. Another handler had watched CD. He had seen how exceptional his skills were at hunting and how protective he had been. He asked if he could work with CD rather than having him taken out of the program. After some lengthy negotiation, they gave him two weeks to see what he could do. CD had a new handler, Rog.

In that two weeks, Rog worked CD harder and longer than any of the other dogs being trained. When it came time to test, CD excelled at searching. He could find bombs and electronic equipment and seemed to be able to expect things before they happened.

CD was given to Rog as his handler on a permanent basis, and they quickly earned a name for being the team you wanted on a mission. The unit they were assigned to twice came under attack, and CD saved two members of the unit.

Dog and handler were inseparable and best friends. When Rog met Jen, CD seemed a little jealous. He would whimper to get attention. It wasn't long, however, until Jen won over CD, and they became a threesome.

On one assignment, Jen and Rog were investigating a man who was selling military guns and ammunition. Jen had been able to track his bank records and found large payments made in a foreign bank. Rog and CD found the guns stored in a storage unit rented by the man. Before they could arrest him, he had found out they were investigating him. He followed Jen one evening and came after her with a knife. Rog and CD had been on their way to meet Jen when CD broke from Rog's hands and rushed around the corner of the barracks. CD flew at the man and practically tore off his hand. Jen and Roger were never able to figure out how CD knew she was in danger before he saw Jen or the man.

On that last mission, CD had been shot in the leg. They were able to fix it, and he healed, but he was no longer able to perform at the level necessary for him to be put back in the field. The army decided to retire him. Jen had been shot in the leg. The damage to her had also been severe, so she had decided to take the discharge they offered. When she found out they were retiring CD, she was able to pull some strings, and after several months, she was able to take him. Woman and dog were dedicated to each other.

CHAPTER 17

Zack

Zack was surprised when Jen called and asked him to come over. When he saw her name on the caller ID, he felt his heartrate jump a little. He answered with a smile but quickly realized something was wrong. Her voice sounded stressed. She asked if he would come over when he had time. He told her he could come right away. She volunteered to barbecue some burgers. It was an easy sell.

When he arrived, she greeted him warmly, but he clearly saw something was wrong. She put her fingers to her lips and motioned for him to come over and look under the kitchen counter.

He was surprised to see a surveillance bug and wondered why anyone would want to listen to her conversations.

They went out to the patio. Zack whistled as he looked around. It was a nice, big yard. It had several flower gardens. Some of the flowers were blooming. The yard was backed up to a small forest of trees. The patio was large enough for two tables with chairs and two Adirondack chairs that sat facing the forest. On the left was an area under construction. Jen explained that she was in the process of developing a rock garden.

"Digging in the dirt and planting things is good therapy for me," she said.

She walked over to the barbecue and lit it. She invited him to sit down. She told him she had come home, and CD had found the bug. She explained that she had gotten a picture of the intruder and wondered if there was any way he could have it run for face recognition.

"Why would someone want to listen to your conversations?"

She shrugged and explained there had been some threats because of the work she had done in the military, but since she had arrived home, there had been no indication of anyone looking for her. He wasn't sure she was giving him the whole story.

"Do you think I should take it out or leave it in place?'"

"Well, maybe we can figure out who it is and then give them false information and maybe trap them," Zack suggested. She forwarded a copy of the picture to his phone. He said he would see what he could do.

She brought out the burgers and put them on the barbecue, then went inside to get the potato salad and fixings. They decided to eat in the house and try to act normal, like friends, so anyone listening would not get suspicious.

It turned out to be a delightful dinner as they talked about their family and friends. He mentioned Paulie, and she told him about how they had met and become such good friends.

At nearly ten o'clock, he reluctantly said he needed to get home. She walked him outside and suddenly grabbed him by the shirt and pulled him close.

"We are being watched, so I am going to kiss you and make this look like a date," she whispered.

She proceeded to kiss him. At first it was tentative, and then it became intense. He started to feel a little dizzy. As she pulled way, they both seemed to be off-balance a little. She laughed nervously.

"Will you be OK alone?" he asked with an unusually husky voice.

"Yes. CD and I will be fine. I'll lock up tight."

Reluctantly, he went to his car. He turned and looked at her again. "You're sure?"

She smiled and nodded. She turned, and he watched her walk into the house. It took him a few minutes to get his breathing back to normal.

CHAPTER 18

Jen

Another sleepless night. Who was watching her and why? Was it because of Afghanistan or one of the investigations when she was stateside? There was nothing else she could think of.

At 5:00 a.m., she gave up and got up. Now the favorite part of her day—her Bible studies. She was not a morning person by nature; in fact, she seemed to get her second wind after about ten at night. But when she sat quietly with God and felt His presence and read His Word, she was reminded of what He had done for her, and well, peace settled over her. She knew nothing that happened today could be more than she could handle with God's help.

She showered and got ready for work, then went out on the patio and soaked in the sunrise. It was, indeed, a beautiful day.

Traditionally for Easter, she watched the movie *The Passion of Christ*. It was a hard movie to watch, but she felt she needed to watch it at least once a year to be reminded of the horrible suffering Jesus had gone through for her. This year, several things had happened, and she had not taken the time to watch it. She had mentioned it to Paulie, and he said he wanted to watch it with her. She needed to set a date for them to do that. Maybe she would invite Zack.

In those months in Afghanistan, there had been so much misery and pain. The people were struggling in their war-torn world and seemed so hopeless. She prayed all the time, for the safety of all those in the military with her and the people of the country who had to live in such a difficult time. She had gotten to know some of the local women and had a chance to witness her faith to them. Two had accepted Christ. It was much different for them when they accepted Christ. They did not live in a country that allowed people to believe what they wanted. They would be persecuted and even killed by their family and friends if they were found out. These beautiful women had shined when they finished their prayer and asked Jesus to be their Savior.

She heard from those women from time to time, when they could send a message through email. The women had started an underground church that now had 107 members.

Tears filled Jen's eyes as she thought of these brave women. She prayed for their safety and for their continued work.

Jen left the house and went to the Coffee Hut. When she walked in, Deb went up to her and said, "OK, details on the dreamy officer. Tell me how you know him—and details, girl, details."

CHAPTER 19

Zack

Zack's mother was his hero. His father died when he was seven and his brother was five. His mother had worked full-time for an accountant and then did bookkeeping for several businesses in Hamilton. Between what Social Security paid and her job, they lived comfortably but with no extras. His mother had made sure they had the necessities, but more importantly, she spent time with her sons. Sunday was family day, and after church each Sunday, they spent time together. Sometimes they went for drives, and sometimes they played games at home. Sometimes they went to the lake and swam, and sometimes they would explore new places in the mountains.

He had several aunts and uncles, and they also made sure to spend time with Zack and his brother, Jake. Zack had loved being an older brother. Even in high school, the brothers hung out together. Sometimes kids at school would tease them because their sports equipment was often a hand-me-down from one of their uncles, or they didn't have all the extras that kids thought everyone should have. There were no Xboxes or motorbikes, but Jake and Zack stuck together.

Jake had been smaller than Zack, and sometimes the older boys would tease him, but they soon learned not to mess with him, because Zack was not smaller, and his punishment for teasing his brother was severe. Zack was also known to take on numerous bullies when they were teasing or hurting someone smaller or more helpless.

Zack's mother's oldest brother had been in the military. He had taught Jake and Zack to hunt and fish. He instilled in them a love for their country and their family. Zack joined the service and later became a Ranger, because that was what his uncle had done.

Jake tried to enlist in the army, but he had a heart murmur, so they said no. Instead, Jake went to college and became a mental health counselor, moved to Missoula, and worked with troubled boys. Not long after that, his mother moved to Polson to be closer to one of her lifetime friends.

Zack liked the military; he liked the prestige of being a Ranger. He met Tamara during his second tour. She had seen him in uniform and sought him out. Her father had been a wealthy banker, and she ran with a crowd of the privileged. It was nice for Zack to see the nicer things in life, but he always felt her friends did not really accept him. Looking back, he realized she liked showing him off to her friends like he was a trophy. He was stationed in the same town and was usually home for three months and then deployed for three months.

On one deployment, his best friend, a fellow Ranger, was severely injured. Zack was upset and began questioning the meaning of life and what he wanted. Even though his mother had raised him in the church, Zack had not really given God much thought. During the time he spent at his friends' side in the hospital, Zack found himself soul-searching and praying. He sought out the chaplain of their unit, and they had talks that often went late into the night. In the end, Zack turned his life over to Christ. He realized that meant making some changes in his life. This included his relationship with Tamara. He realized their casual sexual relationship was contrary to God. He prayed for God's guidance. He decided that because of their sexual relationship, he needed to ask for her forgiveness and either offer to marry her or break it off. When he returned from deployment, he went directly to her house. When he walked in, he found her in bed with one of her friends. When she saw him and saw he was upset, she mocked him and asked him what the big deal was; it was just sex. He walked out and never went back. To his relief, she had not even tried to contact him.

Later, Zack had written her a letter. He explained that he had come to know Jesus and accept Him as his Savior. He apologized to her for their sexual relationship. He explained that he realized he had not honored her in the way God would want him to. He never heard back.

About that time, his tour of duty was up. He had been contemplating whether to re-up. When he had thought of asking Tamara to marry him, he had decided staying in would not be conducive to a good relationship or building a family.

He realized he wanted a wife and a family. He wanted to raise his children like his mother had raised him. Being in the military would mean being gone for long stretches.

The next week, he received a call from Jake. His mom had had a heart attack. He was able to get leave and fly home. The doctors informed them that it was a mild heart attack, and with a change in diet and lifestyle, she should recover completely. Zack realized he wanted to come home and spend time with his mother and brother. He had missed them.

On his way back to base, he had a long layover in Denver. He reached out to the lieutenant he had served under on his first tour. He had retired and settled in Denver and was working for Homeland Security. He met Zack at the airport, where they had lunch and talked. Zack shared his desire to move closer to home but that he didn't know what he would do if he got out. The lieutenant told him about Homeland Security and opportunities it offered. With Zack's two tours in the military, he could join and pretty much pick where he wanted to go. When they said goodbye, Zack had promised to keep in touch.

Over the next couple weeks, Zack did some research on Homeland Security. He found out about their work with human trafficking. He contacted them, went for the initial interview, and liked what he heard. Within two months of his mother's diagnosis, he ended his military career and joined Homeland Security.

He had a two-month break between leaving the military and beginning his training with Homeland. He went home to Montana. He spent most of the time with his mother in Polson and visiting his brother in Missoula. He realized just how much he enjoyed being close to them and having time to reconnect with them. It had been such fun to catch up, and he met Jake's girlfriend. He wanted to be around to share in their lives.

Within six months of completing his training and working out of Seattle, an opening in Whitefish had come up; he quickly put his name in and got it.

Zack had decided that the only way he was going to date was if God put someone in front of him. He wanted his life to be a witness to God and wanted God to guide all his decisions.

CHAPTER 20

Cara

Cara woke to the yelling. It was happening more and more. She heard the man say he had talked with someone, and he could sell Cara for $5,000 and only have to pay $4,000 more for a younger girl. The woman yelled back, "I am not ready to pay four thousand dollars just because you are bored. Buck up and deal with it."

His reply was the new girl would be much younger, so they wouldn't need to get a new one for a long time.

"If she is younger, she won't be able to help around the house, and it will be just another child to take care of."

Cara's heart felt like it had stopped. She covered her ears. "Please, God, if you are there, please don't let another girl have to come here. Please don't let him hurt someone else. And please, God, watch over me and help me."

Cara lay there for a long time after they finished fighting. She knew the next day was not going to be a good one. Mrs. Jenson was always extra mean to her after they fought. She drifted off to sleep. After her prayer, she felt like God was with her.

CHAPTER 21

Zack

Zack woke up wondering how Jen was. He didn't know if he should have left her when she said they were being watched. How had she known, or had it been an excuse to kiss him? He smiled; she could use whatever excuse she wanted if she would kiss him like that.

He drove to the Coffee Hut for his usual muffin and mocha. Maybe he would change it up today and have a blueberry muffin instead of lemon poppyseed. Maybe he would see Jen. The sun suddenly seemed a little brighter.

When he arrived, Jen and CD were already outside. Her head was leaned back, and she appeared to be enjoying the sun on her face.

She seemed startled when he said hello but then smiled. She invited him to join them. He ordered his coffee and came back out to the table where they sat.

"What made you think someone was there and watching?"

She paused. "Why don't you come over tonight? I'll show you. I have a stew cooking in the Crock-Pot."

He nodded and felt a little stirring. He liked that he would see her tonight and felt a little lightheaded as he remembered the kiss. He had never felt this way. Usually, it was just attraction and then going from there.

Zack had not looked for a church since arriving in Whitefish, so he asked if she knew of any good ones. She told him she attended the Congregational Church.

They spent the next half hour discussing churches they had attended.

As they walked to the sidewalk and went their separate ways, Zack looked back and saw she was looking back. He tipped his head and smiled. He didn't remember driving the three blocks back to his office.

He had done some research the night before on kinds of surveillance bugs. The one in Jen's house could easily be ordered on the internet. This wasn't much help. He sent the picture Jen had taken of the man and asked the tech team to see if they could come up with anything.

He felt tightness in his chest. What was going on? Was she stumbling into something that she shouldn't be? Was she safe?

He spent the rest of the day working on trying to figure out how the women and children were being transported and how they could figure out what they were using and how to track them.

He had gone to the rest area on the highway and watched but realized that was probably futile. Even if they stopped there, how would he know which vehicles were theirs?

CHAPTER 22

Jen

It had turned out to be a really good day. Her morning had begun perfectly with her God time and then seeing Zack. She wondered how much she should share with him about her surveillance.

When she arrived at the office, she was able to fill rentals for the month of July. That was earlier than usual.

Jen realized she really needed to decide what she wanted to do for work. The rental agency met her minimal needs. Her father had given her the house when he moved, and her car was paid for, so she didn't have a lot of expenses. She had invested and saved most of her wages from the military, but she didn't want to keep dipping into that when an unexpected expense came along. She was good at computers and research. She wasn't sure how she could translate that into an income and keep some of her independence.

She turned on her computer and tried to find Gordon Denver. One of the older ladies from her church, Ingrid, had told her about Gordon and how they had been in love. Her parents had been rigid and had kept her pretty sheltered. Ingrid had met Gordon at her piano lessons when she was sixteen, and they quickly became friends. He liked jazz and modern music. Her parents would only allow her to play hymns. She would go early and listen to him playing, and then he would wait around until she finished.

After the piano lessons were finished, they would walk the long way home. They talked and laughed and shared hopes and dreams. Soon the friendship was blossoming into young love. For the next year, those feelings had grown.

When her parents discovered the relationship, they packed up the family overnight and moved them to Virginia to live with her father's brother. There had been no way for Ingrid to contact Gordon and tell him where she was or what had happened.

Ingrid seemed so sad when she talked about him.

Her parents had pressured her to marry a young man from their church in Virginia. She did not know him very well when they got married. He was shy and quiet. He never really talked or shared with her, and they didn't have the easy camaraderie that Ingrid had experienced with Gordon. They each fulfilled their roles as husband and wife and later as parents. She had learned to love him.

When their third child, Bonnie, was five years old, his job had transferred them to Whitefish. Five months after they arrived, he was killed in a car accident.

They had started going to the Congregational Church when they first arrived. It was different from the church her parents had belonged to. Everyone seemed so happy and friendly. She didn't feel like they were judging them. The worship was about the love of God and His desire to save them. This was very different from the religion she was raised in, with rules and judgments and punishment.

Following her husband's death, the church had surrounded her with love. Her parents had insisted she return to Virginia, but there was something about this church and the freedom of being out from under her parents' thumb that made her decide to stay.

The members had helped her as she planned the funeral. They

offered to take the children while she dealt with all the paperwork she needed to do to settle his estate. They walked alongside her every step of the way as she raised her three children. One of the members had offered her a job and trained her. Several men from the church had included the boys when they took their sons fishing and hunting and camping. They had been wonderful as male role models for her two boys. They had taught them how to be godly men. One of her boys became the much-loved mayor of the town. He was known as a kind and gentle man, fair in all his dealings.

Ingrid's other son had become a doctor. He lived twenty miles away, in Kalispell. Many of the church people had him as their doctor.

The women of the church had stepped up and helped Ingrid with her daughter. When Ingrid had to go to work, one of the women took care of Bonnie at no charge. The woman said she had two daughters, so what was one more? Bonnie had married a local farmer, had three children, and taught third grade.

Ingrid said the members of the congregation had helped her to understand the love of God. She learned that God was not about rules but about His unbounding love. The people had shown her Christ.

One afternoon just after Jen returned to Whitefish, she and CD went for a walk and saw Ingrid clearing her driveway of snow. Jen insisted on helping, and Ingrid demanded she come in for coffee and some recently baked cinnamon rolls. Their conversation had turned to life and faith, and Ingrid shared her story.

Jen was curious about this Gordon Denver and decided to see if she could find out more about him. She wasn't sure if she would share the results with Ingrid, but she was curious.

She found four listings for Gordon Denver. Two were in their thirties—too young to be Ingrid's Gordon. The other two were about the right age.

Jen was interrupted by the phone. There was a broken pipe in one of the rentals. She spent the next couple hours arranging to have the water turned off for a plumber to fix the pipe and for Ike's Restoration to go in and dry out the floors and assess the damage. She arranged for the nice couple to move into one of the other rentals that was available. They were on their honeymoon. This would give them something to talk about and remember on their anniversary in the coming years.

After making the last call, she looked at her watch. It was five thirty, time to get home and get ready for Zack.

It might just be as nice an evening as it was a day.

CHAPTER 23

Zack

It was Friday night. Zack was looking forward to some time off. He hoped to go for a hike and do some fishing on Sunday afternoon. Maybe Jen would want to come along.

His day had been somewhat productive. He had sent the pictures of the man who had broken into Jen's place. He had come up with a plan for tracking traffic coming through but would need to work with the tech people to figure out if it was possible. He talked with two officers from Border Patrol who thought there was a vehicle that was regularly smuggling drugs across the border.

He caught himself whistling as he changed into blue jeans and a T-shirt and then a blue flannel shirt. He was looking forward to dinner with Jen, and he had to admit he was more than a little curious about this security information she said she would share.

He had forgotten the box of chocolates he planned to take with him at the office, so he stopped there on his way. He had a few minutes, so he checked his email. He was startled when he saw that face recognition showed that the man who had broken into Jen's was suspected of being part of a human-trafficking ring in the area. What would Jen have to do with that? Why was he bugging her house?

He drove to her house. When he arrived, Jen opened the door, and CD came running out to greet him. After kneeling and giving CD's ears a good rubbing, he stood and looked at her. She had on jeans and a dark green sweater, and her eyes seemed to sparkle green.

When Jen had seen him get out of the car, she felt her stomach do a flip. He had changed, and how handsome he looked in his casual clothes. His T-shirt under the flannel shirt showed every muscle, and his jeans fit him nicely. He was definitely nice to look at. She opened the door wider so he could come in and motioned to remind him of the bug.

He handed her the box of chocolates. "A man after my heart," she said and smiled. "I thought we would start with the stew and fresh bread from the bakery. The bread is still warm and is making me hungry."

They talked about their day, and Jen shared details about her search for Gordon. Jen had talked with her father the day before. She told Zack about her father's recent sea fishing trip and how he had been pulled out of the boat by a large, obviously feisty fish. He said he had been worried he might be having a Jonah experience.

Zack insisted on helping her clear the dishes and put them in the dishwasher. He liked the easy bantering they did while working together.

After she started the dishwasher, Jen said, "Let's go outside for a few minutes," but then headed into another room in the house. It looked like a den or maybe a family room. Jen walked up to a bookshelf and pulled out a book, and to his surprise, a door opened, revealing a small room. She motioned for him to follow her.

Inside the room, he saw the monitors along the wall and the computers running programs. On the screen, he could see inside and outside of the house.

Jen explained that there had been threats on her life because of some of the work she and Rog had done. She had worked in intelligence, so after she retired from the army and came to live here, she decided she needed some extra security. She had become less paranoid over the last month and thus had not made sure the security was set when she went to the grocery store the other day. That was the day the man had come into the house and put in the bug.

Zack nodded, a little overwhelmed with the sophistication of the setup. "But how did you know we were being watched the other night?"

Jen went to the monitors and punched in something on the keyboard. The camera narrowed in, and she pushed another button. He saw a slight flicker and heard some frogs croaking and wind chimes tinkling.

"I have perimeter sensor set up sixty yards out. When someone comes into the area, the light flickers and the frog sound emits. Most people don't even notice those because they are so slight. When I am inside the house, there is a tinkling sound like a wind chime to let me know the perimeter has been breached. When we walked outside the other night, I saw two different flickers and heard the frogs."

Zack was extremely impressed. "Did you get an image of their faces?"

She shook her head no. "It was too dark, and they did not come close enough for the cameras to catch them."

Zack pulled out his phone and brought up the picture of the man who had broken into her house. "I got a response from the search just before coming over. Jen, I am worried. This man is thought to be part of the human-trafficking ring we are looking for. The people are dangerous. I don't know why they are targeting you, but I don't like it."

Jen seemed puzzled. "I have no idea. I'll have to see what I can find out." Zack started to speak. "No, I'll be careful, but I want to know who is invading my home."

Zack understood why she wanted to find out who these people were; he would feel the same way. But if they had gone to this much trouble to put surveillance on her, they might be dangerous.

"I won't do anything stupid, but I am going to look into it. My job was in intelligence, and that is what I will do. I don't have access to all the programs and sites that I did, but I might still be able to come up with some things. I will let you know if I find anything."

Zack sighed and resigned himself to the fact that it was the best he could do. She seemed pretty determined, and looking around the room, he realized she was also very capable. He noticed a door on the other side of the small room. Jen saw where his eyes went, so she got up and motioned for him to follow her. She opened the door, and as he stepped through it, he realized he was in what appeared to be her master bathroom. She moved around him and pushed down the towel rack, and the door closed.

"Very impressive."

She smiled and led him into the living room. There was a leather couch, two chairs, and a large television screen. On one end of the room was a sound system. Jen pushed a button, and music came on. They spent the next couple hours visiting and getting to know each other better. He finally said it was time to go.

Jen mentioned sharing spaghetti and watching the movie *The Passion of Christ* the following Sunday, inviting him to join her and Paulie. He was a little surprised at how warm he felt about the idea of sharing more time with her. He agreed—if he could bring the wine. She nodded, and her face lit with a smile. He wished he had a camera and could catch that smile in a picture.

They walked out to his car and said good night. He asked if she would like to go for a hike and do some fishing the next day. She seemed disappointed and said that she had already made plans to spend the afternoon with one of the ladies from her church. She asked for a rain check. When they arrived at his car, his thoughts went back to the last time he was there and that amazing kiss; he wished he could repeat it. When he looked into Jen's face, he thought he saw a similar desire.

"Well, um, good night and thank you for a really nice evening. I will see you at church on Sunday." He reluctantly turned and got into his car. She was still outside watching him as he drove away.

CHAPTER 24

Jen

Jen slept well and woke up refreshed, with Zack on her mind. She got out of bed and stretched. She quickly made her bed and brushed her teeth.

She had thought he might kiss her on Friday night; he looked like he wanted to. It had been a pleasant evening. She had enjoyed his stories. He was easy to talk with, and they seemed to have a lot of similar interests. He had come to church yesterday. He arrived late and sat in the back. She had been disappointed that she did not have time to visit with him.

All day Saturday, she had contemplated what it meant that the man who had broken in was from the human-trafficking gang. She would do some more research on them today and see what she could come up with. She also wanted to find out more about Gordon Denver.

She finished her Bible study and showered. She chose comfortable charcoal slacks and a blue sweater. The weather was getting warmer, but the light sweater should keep her comfortable, and she wouldn't have to wear a jacket.

She set out for work, thinking she would stop by the Coffee Hut and probably see Zack, but then she got two phone calls regarding some problems at a rental. She went straight into the office, and it took the entire morning to get things straightened out. She didn't mind the work, but she did not feel she was working with the talents God gave her.

Jen walked CD and was getting ready to pick up a salad for lunch when her phone rang again. It was her father. He had called recently, so she was surprised to hear from him. He sounded strained but said he was OK. Finally, after him talking for fifteen minutes, she asked him what was going on. She could tell something was on his mind. After a long pause, he said that someone had stopped by his house the day before. Mary had been home alone. The man had said he was a military friend and asked for Jen's current address. Mary had given it to him. When she had asked his name so she could tell Jen he had stopped by, he told Mary he wanted to surprise Jen and left. Something about it had made her father uncomfortable. Jen knew his law enforcement training would have kept him from telling anyone how to reach her, but Mary was much more trusting. She assured her father she would keep a lookout.

After she hung up, she had several more phone calls, and by the time she was finished, it was four o'clock. Her stomach growled. She decided to close the office, go home, and heat up some leftovers.

She thought of Zack and wondered if he had missed her at coffee that morning.

CHAPTER 25

Zack

Zack had met Jake at his mother's Sunday afternoon. Jake's girlfriend was out of town, so the three of them played games and talked. It had been a good visit. Several times, he found himself distracted by the thought of Jen and his investigation. He had told them about Jen. His brother just grinned, and his mother insisted she wanted to meet her.

Zack shared with them that he was working on trying to break up a trafficking ring. Jake sadly shook his head. "The victims are probably going to have a long road back to healing. If there is anything I can do or any way I can help, let me know."

Today, he was pacing his office with frustration. He was not making much headway and was concerned for Jen, wondering if the bug was a part of this. He had hoped to see her at coffee and warn her to be careful, but she had not come in. He hung around for lunch and didn't see her either. Was she avoiding him? Was she somehow involved? That didn't make sense though because the man had broken into her home, and she had given the picture to help identify him.

His phone rang, a call from the district attorney's office in Washington. They were calling regarding the last case he had worked. He was going to have to go testify on Wednesday, and they were preparing him for his testimony. He had caught a man who had kidnapped five children and was holding them in a closet until he could sell them. There had been a fire in the building, and people had seen the man leading the children out of the apartment. Zack had been able to determine he was the kidnapper and eventually found where he had taken the children after the fire. The youngest child was a three-year-old girl. When they raided the house where he was keeping them, Zack found the children and picked up the little girl; she clung to his neck. He rode back in the van to the office, and only when the little girl's parents arrived did she let go of his neck. The man had shown no remorse. Zack hoped he would be in prison for an exceedingly long time, and he was going to do whatever he could to make that happen. He spent the rest of the day reviewing his records to prepare for the testimony.

He had to fly out the next day and testify on Wednesday or possibly Thursday. He needed to meet with John, his supervisor, on Friday and then fly home Saturday. He was looking forward to spending time with Jen and Paulie on Sunday.

He took out his phone and texted Jen. "I'm sorry I didn't see you today. I missed you. I have to go to Seattle for a few days and won't be back until Saturday. Really looking forward to seeing you Sunday in church and watching the movie Sunday night." He had hoped to tell her in person but guessed the text would do.

He went home, fixed dinner, packed, and went to bed early. His flight would be leaving at seven. Fortunately, it was only a fifteen-minute drive to the airport.

CHAPTER 26

Jen

It seemed like a long week. She had been disappointed when she got Zack's text. She missed seeing him and wondered how this man who had come into her life such a short time ago could take up so many of her thoughts. She cleared her desk and rose to leave. She needed to stop by and make a deposit. Then she and CD would head home.

The next morning, Jen changed into comfortable yoga pants and a loose top and went out to work in the yard. She moved dirt and put down a weed barrier, then started hauling rocks over to begin building the rock garden. After three hours, she decided it was as far as she could go before she moved some of the big rocks.

She showered and changed and decided to start the spaghetti sauce and let it simmer in the crockpot. It was always better the second day. The remainder of the day, she spent doing housework and laundry.

Sunday, she woke and got ready for church. She was looking forward to seeing Zack. The service was lively, and Pastor Ken always gave her something to think about. She had lots of friends who attended the church as well. It reminded her of *Cheers*, a place where everybody knew your name.

They had decided to meet early to watch the movie, and they would eat when it was over. When she got home from church, she changed clothes and made the salad. While thinking of the movie, she thought of several years ago when she and Rog had gone to a Maundy Thursday dinner with a Christian Jew friend they had met. He had taken them through the Seder Supper. Jen had been amazed by all the symbolism he had explained. It wasn't until then that she really understood that Thursday dinner that Jesus shared with His disciples before He was arrested. It had been a wonderful evening filled with learning, friendship, fun, and laughter.

She finished making the salad and checked on the spaghetti sauce. She had the pot ready for the spaghetti. The table was set.

She finished up the laundry. She went to the safe room and started looking over some of the results of the searches. Zack had given her the name of the man who broke into her house. She saw he had been arrested on some minor charges and that his address showed he lived in Helena. She looked at the clock and realized she had been there for a couple hours. She jumped up and went to her bedroom. She contemplated brushing her hair and putting on lipstick when she heard the chimes letting her know someone was out front. She moved to the door to welcome them.

Paulie was the first to arrive. He was excited and getting ready to tell her something when Zack arrived.

They moved to the family room. They were all somber as they watched the movie. Jen noticed that each of them were wiping tears from their eyes as they watched the horrible beatings that Jesus took and as He stumbled to where He would be crucified. Through her tears, she noted tears were flowing down Zack's face as well. When the movie was finished, they sat quietly.

"It always amazes me that He would do this for me," Jen commented. Paulie and Zack nodded.

"I'm glad He is my Savior," Paulie said. "Jen, I remember when you first told me about Jesus and took me to Sunday school. I remember when you first helped me pray and accept Him as my Savior. Jen, thank you for that."

Jen reached out and gave Paulie a hug. He usually didn't like hugs, but he tolerated them because he knew Jen loved him and needed to hug him sometimes.

The next hour was spent eating and talking. She liked that Zack seemed comfortable with Paulie.

As they were finishing dinner, Paulie stood up and got their attention. He said in his Paulie way, "I have been doing some work, and I am getting some information for you so you can stop the human trafficking. I will have it to you by Wednesday."

Jen and Zack looked at each other with a start. They both realized the bug was still there under the counter and that it probably had something to do with the human-trafficking ring.

They tried to act natural and quickly ushered Paulie into the family room. They explained about the bug and told him they were fearful that the people had heard him and might come after him. As they talked, Zack's thoughts went back to when they were having pizza and Jen had talked about the human-trafficking information she had found out. He remembered the man who seemed to be listening a little too closely. As they talked, they realized it was the next day the bug had been placed in her house.

Zack and Jen warned Paulie and wanted him to stay with Jen. She was worried they might try to do something to Paulie. Paulie reminded Jen he had a safe place and that he was careful. They could not persuade him to stay somewhere else.

It had been one of the nicest evenings Jen could remember. She felt so much peace.

When she said goodbye to Paulie, she reminded him again to be incredibly careful and to watch out. He smiled and said, "I remember our code, Jen. It will be OK."

As she prepared for bed that night, she said a prayer of thanksgiving and added a prayer for protection for Paulie.

CHAPTER 27

Paulie

Paulie's mother, Doreen, was the granddaughter of a wealthy surgeon. She had been a noticeably quiet girl. Her parents died from a boating accident when she was six. Her grandmother had died by that time, and her grandfather raised her. He was a wealthy surgeon. He worked long hours, so he hired a nanny to take care of her. Her grandfather had made the decision to have her tutored. When she turned eighteen, she went to college. She was awkward in social settings because she had been so isolated growing up. There was another student, Thomas, who was awkward with people, and they had gravitated to each other. When they completed college, they decided to get married. He was an engineer, and she was a botanist. Both were quiet people, so they had little interaction with others. Doreen's grandfather died when she and Thomas had been married just a few years. Her grandfather had left a trust and the house for Doreen.

Doreen had Paulie when she was in her midforties. There was concern because of her age. When Paulie was two years old, they had him tested and determined he had Asperger's syndrome. They had doted on Paulie, but because they were reclusive, he had few social interactions. Doreen and Thomas died in a car accident when Paulie was in his second year of college. He graduated with a mechanical engineering degree.

He and Jen had been friends all through school. She had been stateside when his parents died. She was able to take leave and came home for the funeral to be with Paulie.

Today

Paulie had spent the day watching the parking lot by his house. He was looking down from the second story. It was a busy parking lot right off Highway 93, which came from the south and went right on up to Canada. Most people who came into town drove by the parking lot or stopped to go to one of the stores in the mini mall. Paulie had been sitting at his window several hours a day for several weeks. He used his binoculars and noted the cars coming and going.

Yes, he thought; he had all he needed. It was time to tell it to Jen or her nice friend Zack. He started to turn away and saw two men heading for his house. They didn't look happy, and they didn't look nice.

Paulie quickly went downstairs. He went to the bookcase and moved the book, and the door opened that led down a flight of stairs. He grabbed his briefcase and quickly went down the stairs, closing the door behind him.

When he had seen Jen's special room, he told her he wanted one. She had helped him build it. He lived in the house where he had been raised. It was a house too big for him, but it was home, and he wanted to stay. After they had finished the room, Paulie had moved several pieces of furniture in to make it comfortable. Paulie spent a lot of evenings in this room. Sometimes, when things got too busy or too upsetting for him, he would go into the room, close the door, and just feel safe.

He closed the door just as he heard someone pounding on his door. He went to the monitor that Jen had installed for him. He watched the two men. They pounded on the door again, and then one of the men took something from his pocket and opened his door. They went around the house looking for him and then started going through his things. He had a desk that had been his father's. Paulie didn't use it much; in fact, the papers and books on it had been there since his father died. The cleaning lady would come in and clean and dust, but Paulie did not allow her to throw anything away or put it anywhere else. They searched the desk and threw papers all around the room. They went room to room, looking through everything and throwing papers and books everywhere.

Paulie started getting anxious and rocking. What should he do? What should he do? What if they found him? His rocking got faster and faster. Then Paulie saw them put something under his counter and leave. Paulie figured it must be like the bug that Jen had told him they put in her house. Paulie did not know if he called on the phone if they would be able to hear him.

Paulie had heard stories about people being able to copy someone's phone and see and hear things.

"I will use our secret code," he said out loud.

CHAPTER 28

Jen

Zack and Jen sat at the Coffee Hut. Jen was drinking an iced breve, and Zack an iced mocha. It had been a couple days since Zack and Paulie had been over for dinner, and when Zack saw Jen leaving the office, he had offered to buy her coffee.

"It was really nice to go to church. Thanks for inviting me. The people seem so genuine. The church has so many types of ministries; everyone can find a place to fit in."

They started discussing the sermon when Jen's phone signaled that she had a message from Paulie. She started to read it and gasped.

Zack looked over and saw the blood drain from her face. He grabbed her hand and asked what was wrong.

"Paulie's in trouble." She showed him the text: "911—I have to go home for a visit. There are people there that listen to me. I am fine. I have some directions for you to take care of my house. Call me when you can talk to me."

Zack looked at Jen questioningly. "What—"

Jen cut him off. "Paulie and I had a code when we were younger. His parents were older, and sometimes Paulie would get overwhelmed. When that would happen, he would send me a nine-one-one message and say he was going home. If his parents saw it, they would not understand it. I knew it meant he was upset, and he was going to his tree house. The tree house fell down several years ago, but I think he is telling me he is in his safe room, and some people came to his house. His statement about people there who listen to me means he thinks someone may have bugged his house. I have to get home and call him." Jen stood up to leave. CD was standing there on alert. He knew something was wrong.

"I'm coming with you. Do we need to go to Paulie's?"

"No, he is telling me to stay away for now. I can use my encrypted phone. I just need to get home to call him."

Encrypted phone? Who the heck was this woman?

Zack got up and went outside with her. His car was in front of the coffee shop, so he motioned for her to get in. "This will be faster, and we can come back and pick up your car later." He put CD in the back while he got into the front seat.

When they arrived at Jen's, she jumped from the car, and Zack signaled for her to go ahead while he let CD out. Jen quickly put the code in, opened the door, and headed straight to her safe room. Zack followed. He noted she was doing something on the computer.

"This will make it safe to talk with Paulie even if they have somehow compromised his phone." She pushed in his number. "Paulie, Paulie, it is OK. Tell me what happened." Jen listened for a few minutes. "Do you feel safe, Paulie? Are your sure you want to stay there?" Jen relaxed and then perked up. "OK, OK, just a minute." She grabbed a paper and pen and handed it to Zack. "Write this down. OK, Paulie, Zack is here with me, and he will write everything down." Jen started repeating letters and numbers, and Zack quickly jotted them down. There were twelve sets of letters and numbers.

"OK, Paulie, I am going to talk with Zack about these, and I will see what we can do. It might take a few days. Are you OK with staying where you are? Do you have enough to eat and drink? Are you going to be OK?" She nodded. "Send me another message if you need anything. I will check in every day."

Jen turned to Zack. "Those are license plates of vehicles that may be transporting people for human trafficking. Paulie has been watching traffic for the last few weeks. He has seen a pattern of these vehicles that have come through on a regular basis, and he said there are always two men driving them. The windows are blacked out, and they were either vans or trucks. They would stop in the parking lot, and after a little while, two other men would pull up. They would switch vehicles and drive away."

"Has Paulie been writing these down? If they searched his place, they may have found the list."

Jen shook her head. "He did not write down anything. He memorized them."

"Ahh, Jen, I am sorry, but I don't think that is very reliable."

"Let me tell you more about Paulie. Paulie's parents were in their sixties when Paulie was in high school. They never traveled outside of Whitefish. I had always been interested in how Paulie could remember numbers, so I decided to try an experiment, just to test him. My dad had helped me buy a Chevy Nova when I was a junior so I could get back and forth to my job. One day, I decided to take Paulie on a drive. I drove to Polson down the east side of the lake and back up on the west side. I knew he had never seen the signs on the road because he had never traveled that way. Then a couple weeks later, I told Paulie we were going to go driving again. I asked him to repeat each sign we passed. He could not remember what they advertised, but he remembered each phone number. About half a mile before the sign, I would ask him what the sign said and what the phone number was. I had not told him I was going to do this. I wanted to see if he could remember the numbers. Paulie got every number right on every sign we had passed, in every direction we had gone. He could even tell me what mile markers they were close to."

"Savant memory," Zack said.

"Yes—and always right."

CHAPTER 29

Zack

Zack had gone back in the office and run each of the license plates. He called his supervisor. He went home to try to get some sleep, but it was worthless. At three in the morning, he finally got up and went to the office. He got the results of the license plates and started looking for the kind of vehicles they were. At six, he called his supervisor. It was a good thing he was an early riser. They discussed how to proceed. He hung up, yawned, and looked at his watch. It was 6:44; good—the coffee shop would be open. He grabbed his jacket and walked the few blocks to the Coffee Hut.

Just as he turned the corner, he saw Jen and CD get out of the car. She waved and released CD. CD went running to Zack. Zack stopped to pet him and then continued walking toward Jen. CD walked next to him.

"Wow, you are up early today."

"Yeah, I couldn't sleep, and CD was restless, so I decided to get coffee and take CD for a walk. Then I was going to stop by your office to see if you found out anything. You look like you have not slept all night."

Zack explained the process of running the plates and looking for common owners and then putting the computer to work to find commonalities. He told her he had spent several hours on the phone with his boss last night, deciding how to proceed.

"If you find that they are part of the ring, you won't be able to just pick them up. If you pick up one, the message will get around, and they will shut down their operations or do something different. You need to figure out how to catch them all at once."

Zack just nodded; he was amazed at how she had recognized the problem. While he knew he wasn't supposed to comment on an ongoing investigation, he would have liked to talk it through with her.

He reached over and opened the door to the Coffee Hut. Their senses were assaulted with the smell of freshly brewed coffee and cinnamon rolls. They took a breath at the same time and said, "Mmm." His stomach grumbled, so he ordered coffee and each of them a cinnamon roll.

After ordering, they sat at a table in the corner. CD sat at Jen's feet. She was deep in thought. Then, as if talking to herself, she said, "I need to talk with Paulie and see if we can narrow down the days and times he saw the vehicles. With that, we could run an algorithm to see what kind of pattern is there, if there is one. Then we could try to find a way to track them and see if a pattern develops. Once we have a pattern, you might be able to plan a way to catch most or all of them at the same time and shut the operation down. Also, we could run the owners and see if they have other vehicles registered to them. My guess is that they will be under corporations."

"You can do that? The algorithm and check for a pattern, I mean?"

Jen smiled and explained her job with army intelligence was mostly that kind of thing, both when she was stateside and deployed. "We watched with satellites, looked for patterns, and then predicted what would happen next. We monitored telephones, radio, social media, and other ways of communication."

Zack saw what a tremendous help that would be. As he was taking the last drink of coffee, he sat up straight. "What if I could talk with my boss and see if we could hire you as a consultant? With your background and expertise, it could speed things along. I can do some of the basic computer work, but often I have to wait until the tech people can get to my work. Would you be interested?"

"Do you think they would let me do that?"

Zack could hear the excitement in her voice. "I'm going back to the office to contact my boss. I don't know how long it will take or even if they will consider it, but I will call you when I find out."

"In the meantime, I'm going back to the house to call Paulie."

CHAPTER 30

Paulie

Paulie looked around his safe house. It was built in the basement of his house. It was a twenty-by-twenty-foot space. He entered it by going behind the secret bookcase in the den and down some stairs. At one end was a television and two comfortable chairs. There was a small table with two chairs, a refrigerator, and a microwave on one side. Next to that was a small countertop with storage for some dishes and food. In the middle of the opposite wall was a built-in desk and two computers. The computer screens were split into six sections, showing pictures streaming from the cameras around the house. There was a camera in each room and two outside, one showing his walkway and the other showing the street. He could see if anyone was coming or going. On the other side of the room was a small bathroom, much like that of a motorhome. He had to sit on the toilet to take a shower.

Paulie liked it here. It was safe, and he enjoyed the quiet. He missed windows and sunshine, but the two computers bringing in live feed kept him from feeling cut off.

He was thinking he needed to sneak upstairs today and get some more clothes. The ones he stored down there wouldn't last much longer. He didn't dare wash clothes; bringing more down seemed to make more sense.

Sometimes when Paulie got anxious, he went into his little bathroom, shut the door, and rocked. His anxiety would ease, and he would come out.

He spent his days reading, watching TV, and working. Paulie worked for a company that published technical how-to instructions. He would pick up a large stack of manuscripts, read and edit them, and then turn them in and pick up the next batch. His mind for details and his engineering degree helped him picture whatever was being described. He was able to catch errors that someone else might not. As he read through the instructions, he could picture each step in his mind as if he were doing it. He was able to add information or clarify steps to make it easier for the consumer to use. He had just picked up ten manuscripts two days before the men had come to his house. Fortunately, he had grabbed them when he came into his safe room.

He was editing some instructions on how to build raised gardens using pallets when his phone rang. It was Jen. He knew it would be safe to answer if she was calling.

"Jen, hi. Did Zack check out the license plates?"

They talked about what Zack had been doing, and Jen got more information about the vehicles, the times of days, and exact locations where they parked. Paulie was able to tell her the color and type of each vehicle.

"You are amazing, Paulie. You know that, right?"

"I know that I have a very good memory and that …"

"It's OK, Paulie. I didn't really expect you to answer that. Are you OK? Do you need anything? Food, books, soda? It might be a little while before it is safe for you to come out and be seen around town."

Paulie assured her he was fine. They spent the next several minutes discussing some groceries he would like and how Jen would get them to him. They decided she would go over later that afternoon.

He was looking forward to seeing her.

CHAPTER 31

Jen

Jen and CD stopped by Zack's office to check on the progress. He filled her in on what he had been doing so far. He had asked his boss about her consulting and helping. He said he should know by this evening if they were going to bring her on board.

Zack cautioned Jen that finding a way to break up the ring might take a few weeks. They would need to plan and coordinate the takedown to get the largest possible number of people. Paulie would not be safe until then. He had cleared it with his boss to take him to a safe house.

Jen shook her head. "I don't think he will go. He has lived in his house since he was born. It is a safe place for him, and he doesn't do well with change. I am going to see him in a little while, but I will run it by him and see what he thinks."

"Is it safe to go see him? Can he live in the safe area for an extended period?"

"I have a plan on how I can get into the house and fool the

people listening. I won't be able to spend much time with him, but I can see how he is doing."

"I have requested a couple of guys from the state police to keep an eye on his place, monitoring any coming and goings. They will make sure he stays safe."

They arranged to meet for dinner, and Jen left to go see Paulie.

Before Jen went to the grocery store, she stopped by the house and picked up some suitcases. She thought it would look less suspicious than bags full of groceries if someone was watching her go into the house. She stopped by the grocery store and bought him some fresh vegetables and apples (his favorite, Granny Smith). She added a couple of videos she thought he might like and impulsively got him two kinds of ice-cream bars. She smiled. He always got excited when he saw the Magnum ice-cream bars. She put the groceries into the suitcases and drove over to Paulie's house.

She used the key he had given her to let herself in. When she walked in, she gasped. It was a mess. She took out her phone and acted as if she was calling the police. She explained that she had come to her friend's house to drop off some suitcases she had borrowed and water his plants because she knew he was out of town. The house had been broken into, and things were scattered all over. She stopped as if to listen. "I can't tell if anything is missing, and he is out of town for a couple of weeks. Do you think it would do any good if I came to the station to fill out a report?" She paused. "No, I can't think of anyone who would do this. There have been other break-ins?" Another pause. "Would it be OK if I just cleaned it up a little? I would hate to have him come back to a mess like this." She paused again. "OK, I will call him and see if he is OK with me picking some of the mess up, and if so, I will do that. I will stop by when I am done and make a report."

She waited for a minute and then pretended to call Paulie. "Paulie, hi." Pause. "I just came to your house to check your plants, and someone broke in. Your things are all over. Nothing seems broken, but it is a mess." Pause. "It's OK, Paulie. I called the police and reported it. They said there have been some other break-ins in the area. I will stop by and fill out a report, but they said there was not much they could do." Pause. "I told them you were gone for a couple of weeks." Pause. "No, I don't think you need to come home unless you want to. I'd like to clean up the mess if you are OK with that." Pause. "No, I don't mind."

Jen walked around, picking things up and straightening a few things. CD followed her as she took the suitcases over to the bookcase, then went to the closet and took out the vacuum. She turned it on. Next, she went to the bookcase and tipped the book. It opened. She hauled the suitcases downstairs. Paulie was excited about the ice-cream bars but even more excited to see CD. He thanked her for the groceries. They decided he would go upstairs and get some clothes while she was cleaning so the vacuum would continue to cover the sounds he might make. She warned him it was pretty messed up, but he reminded her he had watched the monitors and seen them do it. Jen went up with him and cleaned while he got his things. They returned to the safe room.

"Paulie, this might take a few weeks, and I think it is going to be hard for you to stay down here that long. Zack has arranged for you to go to a safe house if you are willing."

"Jen, this is my home. I think I would be scared to go anywhere else."

Jen told him she planned to clean up a little more and then leave. She promised to call the next day and got his promise that he would text her if he needed anything or if he needed to talk.

She left his house, stopped by the police station, and made the report. She knew they would be unhappy that she had not called them to come to the house, but she didn't want to take the chance of anyone discovering Paulie, which is why she had faked the phone call to them in the first place. They scolded her for not calling before she cleaned up. She acted surprised and said she was sorry.

She was running a little late, so she sent a quick text to Zack as she stopped in her driveway. She went in and washed her face. She decided to put on a little eye shadow and mascara. Then she changed into some gray slacks and an apricot top. She grabbed a jacket and hurried out the door.

When she arrived at the Pizza Station, she noticed Zack's SUV in the parking lot. She left CD in the car and walked in. It took her a minute to spot him. He was in a corner in the back. He stood as he saw her, and she liked the smile of welcome on his face. Her stomach did a little flip, and she was glad she had taken the time to change and put on a little makeup.

He nodded to a chair as she came closer and waited for her to sit first.

"I hope you are OK with the table. I thought it would give us a little more privacy."

They took a minute to study the menu and decided on a combination of pizza and beer.

After the waitress left, Zack told her about his conversation with his boss. They had decided they would contract with her to help with the case. "My boss was pretty impressed with your credentials and experience. He said he talked to your commander, who sang high praises of you."

Jen told him what a great man her commander was and how he took personally each mission and the safety of everyone involved. Zack outlined what her job would be and the compensation they were offering. She enthusiastically agreed to the contract terms, and they toasted to working together.

When their food arrived, they ate, discussed books, and argued over who the best author was. Then they discussed a movie they each were looking forward to seeing.

After the waitress took away their plates, they spent the next one and a half hours talking about the investigation and what they were going to do.

He walked her out to the car and opened her door. When he reached over and touched her arm, she felt shivers run up it. The he leaned down and kissed her—a short kiss but a kiss with promise.

"Just in case someone is looking." He smiled. "See you tomorrow."

Jen drove home feeling a little giddy. It had been a nice kiss. She hoped it was not just because someone might be watching.

CHAPTER 32

Trevor

The Shed was part of a complex on an old army base. At one end of the complex were barracks that the boys slept in. They were heavily guarded. Another part of the complex held the training grounds. This was where the boys were taught skills in combat. The last part of the complex was a large arena. More than forty boys lived in the complex. They were groomed to fight. Once a week, eight of the boys were led to the arena. The arena looked like a miniature coliseum with ten-foot walls surrounding it. Seating above the arena could hold fifty to sixty people.

Two at a time, the boys were forced to enter the arena. The instructions were to fight. The winner would receive two days of any food they chose, a female or male companion, and a cash award. This would buy items from the commissary. The loser, if he lived (which occasionally they did not), would live in isolation for those two days, with only bread and water.

Trevor had trained for six weeks before he entered his first fight.

He lost. He ended up with a twisted wrist and some cracked ribs. After he got out of the two days of isolation, they had sent him to the infirmary, where they wrapped his wrist and taped his ribs. He had resumed training two days later.

The anger in Trevor burned stronger and stronger. He learned to use it when he fought. When he went into the ring, he exploded with his anger and took it out on his opponent. He quickly learned to shut out the noise of the spectators and their demands for more blood. Each time he won, the next opponent was more difficult. He won more fights than he lost. He enjoyed the food after the fights but refused any sexual companionship or drugs that were offered for the first four fights. Finally, he agreed to a female companion. When she came in, she looked so scared. She was probably about thirteen years old. They spent the evening talking. Trevor found out she had been kidnapped when she was younger, but when she turned twelve, the man who had bought her said she was ugly and old, so they sold her to her current master. He made her perform sex with whomever he said. Each time Trevor won after that, he asked for her. They spent the night talking.

CHAPTER 33

Zack

Zack spent the next day working with his supervisors and members of the task team that had been set up to take down the human-trafficking ring. He arranged for Jen to have all the passwords and codes she would need.

There were a lot of license plates on Paulie's list, and they had to try to figure out how to track them and predict where they would be at a certain time. Then they needed to coordinate on a time to intercept as many of them as possible to prevent them from going underground. They needed to do it quickly. The sooner they were able to stop these criminals, the less likely more women and children would be harmed. The more women and children that were saved resulted in less heartache and devastation for the family and friends of the victims.

Zack knew well the extreme heartache that resulted when his friend had been kidnapped. He and Toni had been as close as sister and brother. At first, they thought she was with friends and had lost track of time. It wasn't until evening that they started calling around, and she was nowhere to be found. The family did not have much money but waited with the police, hoping for a ransom call. None ever came. After two months, her body had shown up in a town four hundred miles away. The FBI and local law enforcement had worked together. They determined she had been kidnapped, probably by men who were planning to use her for human trafficking. Several months later, the authorities caught a break in the case when they found several other girls who had been kidnapped around the same time. From what they had been able to determine, Toni had fought them and eventually escaped, only to be caught and killed. Her death had been used as a warning to the other girls.

Zack remembered the hopelessness of not knowing what had happened to her. When her body had been found, the pain and anguish the entire family experienced was excruciating. Her parents never recovered. Eventually, they divorced, and her father became an alcoholic. He died in a car accident almost exactly three years after her abduction. Her mother became reclusive and suffered from anxiety. She became so agoraphobic that she had not come out of her house for eight years. Zack realized how much this had affected him when Tamara had not come home from a vacation the day she said she would, and he had freaked out. She had called him and told him later, but only after he had spent eight hours panicking. He wasn't sure if he would ever get over that feeling.

He knew God was in control and that God would get him through anything, but he never wanted to experience that fear and helplessness again. He gave himself a shake and called Jen. He arranged to meet her at her house so he could get her started on the computer work they needed from her.

He stopped by the Coffee Hut, picked up coffee, and headed over.

As he pulled up, Jen was already waiting for him at the door. She had on a running suit the color of her eyes. When she looked at him, he could see her excitement. He hoped at least part of it was at seeing him and not just the case. He remembered the quick kiss of the night before and how he had wanted it to be much more.

They walked around to the patio.

"I think we need to discuss the surveillance bug in your house. Do we want to accidently discover it, or do you think we might be able to use it to feed them false information?"

"Let's keep it. We don't want them to know we have found it. We can feed them false information. It might help when the time comes to catch them off guard and make it easier to catch them. Sort of like herding cattle."

Zack chuckled; he liked the way she thought. "Let's plan on that."

They finished their coffee and moved into her safe room. She started her computers, and he gave her the information she would need to set up accounts and access the numerous programs she would need. Zack had her complete the paperwork needed to bring her on board. Her high security clearance from when she was in the military was still good, so the process was shorter than it might have been.

"With these programs, I can tap into camera feeds at various places around the country and see if I can pick up the vehicles Paulie gave us. I will write an algorithm that should show us where they go and where they are predicted to go. I am hoping that within a week or two, we should have an idea of how the ring works. If they have a predictable pattern, it should be straightforward. If it varies a lot, it will take longer.

"Fortunately, people like this don't think we will be tracking them and probably won't vary their pattern much. They think they are undetectable. We can keep them thinking that way by the information we feed them through the bug. We can make them believe we are going about looking for them in an entirely different way. This should give us an element of surprise when the time comes."

Zack nodded and asked if he could pray for them, the assignment, and that what they were planning would be hidden from those they were trying to catch. Jen grabbed his hand, and he prayed.

Jen turned and looked at him. "I am concerned about Paulie. He is doing OK in his little safe place, but I am not sure how long he can stay there. I am afraid he will start getting restless. I'm not confident he can hold out if this takes longer than a couple of weeks."

They discussed the situation and came up with several options.

"Paulie has always lived in that house. He feels safe there, and he does not like change. If we take him out of there to somewhere safe, it may cause him to panic and create more problems for him. I want to be careful in how often I go over to check on him because I don't want them to become suspicious. I can only come up with a few excuses for when to go to the house and what to do there. I need to figure out ways to create understandable noise so I can sneak into the den and see him. Also, Paulie will be running out of work soon, and if I am seen going in and out with books and papers, they may get suspicious."

Zack understood what Jen was saying but wasn't sure what they could do about it. "Is there a way we can sit down, talk to Paulie, and maybe figure out what he wants? I have the approval to take him to a safe house if he is willing."

"Let me think about it for a while."

They moved into the kitchen, and Jen made coffee. They talked about their day and then talked about how frustrated Zack was about the trafficking ring. They had discussed earlier what they could say to give the listener the impression they had no clue and to make them think they had no information.

When Zack rose to leave, he reached over, pulled her close, and gave her a kiss. When he stepped back, she was smiling.

"See you tomorrow."

CHAPTER 34

Paulie

Paulie looked down at the phone and saw Jen was calling. With relief, he answered it. "Jen, are you OK? Have you figured out what to do? Has Zack arrested them yet?"

Jen explained that they were working on it. She said she and Zack were trying to come up with a plan for how to come to the house and talk with him without making the people listening suspicious. She promised to call him back no later than the next day. He gave her a list of things that he needed picked up from the grocery store.

After hanging up, Paulie paced around the room. Jen had sounded concerned and wouldn't tell him what she needed to talk to him about. He had almost completed all the manuscripts he was working on and was starting to feel a little restless. For the last few days in this safe room, he had spent most of the time working on the books. He wasn't sure what he was going to do when he finished them. He was getting more anxious. He sat down and started rocking. "OK, breathe." Jen had told him God listened to him when he prayed. He had prayed before, and it did seem like God listened, so he prayed. Paulie's prayers were simple. "God, I don't know what to do. I don't know how to help Jen. I know I am starting to have trouble. Help. Amen." He felt calmer when he had finished.

He went to the kitchen area and made a toasted cheese sandwich and apple slices. He turned on music; he liked classical music when he was stressed. As he ate and listened, he began to feel much better. He could do this.

CHAPTER 35

Jen

Jen and Zack came up with the plan that they would act like they were on a date and stop by to water Paulie's plants. They would turn on the music and act like they were dancing and then slip down and see Paulie for just a couple minutes. They planned to encourage him to consider going into protective custody until they were able to make the arrests.

They walked into the house, and Jen said she was just going to water the flowers. Zack turned the music on, and they talked about how nice it was to dance.

They slipped down to see Paulie. Jen saw him start to panic when they told him this might take a few weeks. They explained that it would be best if they moved him to a safe house until it was over.

"This is my home. I've never lived anywhere but here, with all my things. I can't go anywhere else."

"Calm down, Paulie. We can try to come up with another plan if you think you can be OK for a week or so," Jen assured him.

Paulie nodded.

They quickly returned upstairs and left. When they got to the car, Zack grabbed her hand, turned her around, and whispered, "In case anyone is watching," as his lips came down on hers. It started as a gentle kiss and quickly turned Jen's bones to mush. Reluctantly, he pulled away. She smiled as she realized he was breathing as hard as she was.

CHAPTER 36

Zack

Zack was restless throughout the night. He kept remembering the kiss with Jen and each time felt his heart beat a little faster. She was an amazing woman, but he did not have time to think about her; he needed to keep focused on the game plans if they were going to be able to take these jerks down.

At 4:30 a.m., he gave up and got out of bed and spent some time with his Bible. His prayers included guidance for his relationship with Jen and to keep him focused. He prayed they would be able to take this organization down and rescue the victims from the grasps of the sick, evil tormentors.

He went into the office at five thirty. He took out a map and started marking the route they had determined was probably being used. He contacted his boss, who fortunately was an early riser and didn't mind early-morning phone calls. They discussed the progress.

Jen was working on a way to tap into cameras all over the country. She should be able to track some of the license plates. His supervisor reported what they had found when they dug into those to whom the license plates were registered; they were connected to the same shell corporation, Mantake Org. Other vehicles were registered to them as well. It felt like they were on the right track. Paulie's information had been excellent. Jen was in the processes of writing the algorithm that would pick up the vehicles on various cameras. That would give them the information they needed to see if there was a pattern. Fortunately, today there were cameras everywhere—some on stoplights, others on buildings. She would be able to tap into cameras on private property, such as malls and stores. With the program she had written and her access to the various monitoring agencies, she should begin receiving information immediately. Then they should be able to determine the patterns. Unfortunately, Montana did not have as many cameras as other places, but she would still be able to pick up some of the vehicles. Before he left last night, Jen had shown him how they were already getting data on some of the vehicles from Texas, California, and New Mexico.

"When we get ready, we are going to have to try to hit multiple places and vehicles at once so they cannot give warnings to anyone else in their system. This is going to be a logistical nightmare." Zack sighed.

They talked for almost an hour. They arranged a call for the next day and for Jen to be present. She could help them understand her part in how to make this work.

Zack hung up, smiling at the idea of sharing a call—well, sharing just about anything with Jen. Ten minutes later, he was still smiling and looked at the clock to see if it was early enough to go to the Coffee Hut and hopefully see Jen.

CHAPTER 37

Jen

Jen's night had been restless. Each time she closed her eyes, she remembered the kiss from Zack. It had been amazing, but she needed to not read too much into it.

She finally got out of bed at 1:30 a.m. and worked on the algorithm. She felt confident it would work once she had the information from the cameras picking up the license plates. Just as she was walking to the bedroom, she heard the warning that someone or something was outside. She waited but did not hear it again. She went to bed and slept peacefully until 6:00 a.m., when she woke from a dream about Zack and his kiss. She stretched and smiled and decided she needed to get going.

She quickly showered and dressed, then sat down with her Bible. She had been reading 1 John.

> If we say we have no sin, we deceive ourselves and the truth is not in us. If we confess our sins, he is

> faithful and just to forgive us our sins and to cleanse us from all unrighteousness. (1 John 1:8-10)

Jen sat and contemplated the verses. One of her greatest heartaches was Penny, a friend she had made in boot camp. They had stayed in touch and had been stationed at the same base. They often talked about God. Penny said she was a good person and didn't really do much wrong, so she figured she would go to heaven.

Jen had tried to explain that it wasn't enough to be good. We had to be perfect if we wanted to get into heaven on our own, and none of us could do that. The consequence of not being perfect was hell. That is why God had sent Jesus. He paid the price for all our sins because He was God and man. He lived perfectly and then suffered the horrible death and then rose from the grave. If we believe that, we will have eternal life. Penny never seemed to understand, and she had been killed on her next deployment. Jen prayed that in those last hours she might have come to faith in Jesus.

So often she felt haunted by the things that had happened in Afghanistan. It had been a difficult time for her. She was thankful that, while living under the constant threat of death, she had peace, knowing she was in God's arms. The God of angel armies was with her no matter what happened. The months after she was wounded and Rog was killed had been difficult. She held onto God's love and comfort, and it sustained her. She wrote in her journal and thanked God for His protection. She prayed that He would bless their efforts as they tried to stop these horrible people. She thanked God that Rog had a relationship with Him and for the knowledge that she would see him again in heaven someday.

She snuggled with CD for a while and thanked God that he was able to be with her after she got out of the hospital.

She left for work with a little more bounce in her step. She was looking forward to the day. Stopping for coffee was a must, and she was pleased to see Zack there. When she saw him, she lowered her eyes. She wasn't quite sure how to greet him, with the kiss still so fresh in her memory. CD pulled her toward his table, and Zack stood and nodded at the barista. "When I saw you, I ordered your coffee, and they are making it now. I hope that was OK."

Jen smiled. "It's perfect."

Zack filled her in on his conversation with John. They arranged a time to call him the next day. Zack seemed reluctant to go but said he had another appointment, and she had to get into her office.

Jen and Zack had been spending most evenings together, working on the case, watching movies, or just visiting. He said, "I wish I could say we could get together tonight, but I have several things going, and I am not sure what all is going to happen, so I will call you later."

Jen nodded, feeling a little disappointed but totally understanding. She looked forward to seeing him the next day.

She arrived at the office and had several phone calls and problems she needed to deal with. She quickly handled them, and as she finished, her eyes fell on the information about Gordon Denver. The one who seemed to fit the profile lived in Bigfork, a small town less than an hour away. She decided to drive over and see if she could meet with him. This was not the kind of conversation she felt was appropriate for a phone call. "What are the chances, Lord, that these two people fell in love a thousand miles from here and now live forty miles apart? Only You could orchestrate this, Father. Please guide me to what I need to do and say." She added a quick prayer asking God to guide her and Zack and the relationship that appeared to be developing.

CHAPTER 38

Gordon

She stopped by her house and dropped CD off so he would not have to wait in the car; she didn't know how long she would be. She checked to make sure the program was running that was looking for the vehicles they were targeting.

As she drove to Bigfork, she realized it was past lunchtime, so she stopped at the Dairy Queen for some chicken fingers and looked up the directions to his house on her phone. She got back in and drove the three minutes to his house. She knocked several times and turned to leave, thinking no one was home. Maybe God didn't want her to do this.

"Hello," a voice said behind her.

"I'm sorry. I thought no one was home. My name is Jen. Are you Gordon Denver?" He nodded. "I wonder if I could talk with you for a few minutes."

"I was on the back patio and thought I heard the door. Won't you come around and join me for some iced tea?"

As they walked around the house, she admired his flower gardens. They were filled with color and beauty. She told him about her most recent project of building a rock garden. He showed her several flowers that she might want to include.

"Do you have a vegetable garden as well?"

"No. For years when my wife was alive, I had a large garden, but now there is just me, and there just didn't seem to be a reason to grow vegetables when I eat so little."

He offered her a seat and went into the house, returning with iced tea. "Sugar?" Jen declined.

"Mr. Denver—"

"Gordon, please."

"Gordon, do you remember a girl named Ingrid?"

Jen saw him gasp. He sat silently for a minute with his head down. When he looked up, she saw tears in his eyes.

"Ingrid. I have not heard that name in a long time. That was the name of my first true love. I was in high school and fell in love. She moved away suddenly. I never knew where she went, but I have never stopped loving her. I met my wife five years later, and we had a good marriage and two children, but Ingrid has always been in my heart. Where did you come up with that name?"

Jen told him about her conversation with Ingrid. Gordon confirmed he was indeed that person. She explained to him that she lived forty miles away. She asked if he would like to meet her.

"Does she know about me?"

Jen shook her head. "I didn't tell her I was going to look for you because I didn't want her to be disappointed if I couldn't find you. I think she would be extremely excited to see you, but I wanted to talk with you first. She is a wonderful lady who goes to my church. She is loving and kind and a joy to everyone she meets."

Gordon sat there quietly for a few minutes. "I think I would like that. Will you be sure she is OK with meeting me?"

Jen assured him she would. They talked for a few minutes more and exchanged phone numbers. Jen promised to contact him in the next couple of days. As she drove away, she was smiling, and she kept the smile on her face for the next thirty minutes.

CHAPTER 39

Jen

She decided she would stop by Paulie's and check with him to see if he needed anything else. She was concerned; he had seemed anxious last time they talked. She had assured him she would stop by today with groceries.

When she arrived at Paulie's, she went in and turned on the radio, then went to the bookshelf and opened the door to Paulie's safe room. She called his name, but he did not answer. She quickly went in and looked around the room. He was not there. She took out her phone and called Zack.

"I'm at Paulie's, and he is not here. I don't see signs of trouble, but I … Oh, wait. Paulie is on the other line. Hold on.

"Hel—"

"Jen, they are after me. I don't know what to do."

"Slow down, Paulie. What is going on?"

"When you didn't come with the groceries this afternoon, I decided I would just go to the store. I picked up a few things, and when I started to leave, I saw the two men who tore up my house. I am back in the store, but, Jen, what do I do?" Jen could hear the panic in Paulie's voice.

"Take a breath. I am only five minutes away. Go to the Starbucks in the store, order coffee, and sit there. Do not go anywhere. They won't try to take you or hurt you there. I have Zack on hold, so I'll have him meet us there. Paulie, hold on and say a prayer, and I will right there."

She drove quickly to the store. Jen started to blame herself. She should have taken him the groceries earlier. She should have waited to go to Bigfork. The she heard "No condemnation. You did nothing wrong." Jen breathed in slowly. It was just one of those things. Paulie was not patient, she knew that, but he should have waited. She probably should have told him when she was coming. It was too late now; they just had to figure out what to do from here. When Jen arrived, she parked in the handicap parking and ran inside. When she got to Starbucks, she saw two men approaching Paulie, and they didn't look happy.

She rushed over to him. "Hi, Paulie! Welcome home. I hope you had a good visit with your family." Jen hugged Paulie, and as she did, she whispered, "It's OK, we've got you." The two men backed away and stood at the end of the counter.

As they sat down, they saw Zack dressed in his uniform coming toward them. Jen stood up. "Look! Paulie is back from visiting his family."

Out of the corner of her eye, she saw the two men move away and go outside. She let out a breath with a whoosh. She hadn't realized she had been holding her breath.

They sat at the table and talked about what had happened. They were sure the men were from the trafficking ring. They did not know if the men knew Paulie had been staying at home.

"We need to get you somewhere safe, Paulie. It is going to take some time before we can make arrests, and we need to make sure no one can get to you."

Paulie started to resist, but as they talked, he realized Zack had his safety in mind. He reluctantly agreed to go along with his plan.

They discussed how they could get Paulie to the safe house without being followed and what he would need to do. Zack contacted John and arranged for the safe house. John also arranged for an FBI agent to pick up Paulie at the back of the store in an hour. Jen worked with Paulie to make a list of all the things he needed from his house. She smiled when he said his stuffed bear. Whatever would make this easier on him, she would do. They arranged for her to go to the house with Zack and pick up the things on his list. She would pick up the completed manuscripts and drop them off and then pick up any new work. Zack arranged for everything to be delivered to Paulie through several different people, to make sure no one could find out where Paulie was.

They made sure the men were still out front when they slipped Paulie out the back door of the store. Jen and Zack went to his house and picked up all the things on his list, delivered his completed work, picked up the new work, and handed it over to the next person. By the time they were done, it was after 8:00 p.m.

"I don't know about you, but I am starving," Zack said.

Jen nodded. "I think a nice, big burger."

"Sounds like a plan. There is a Red Robin just down the road. How about we go there?"

Jen nodded enthusiastically.

They both downed the burgers in record time. Jen pushed back from the table. "That was so good. I'm glad I got to see you today. I didn't think I was going to." Then Jen remembered her visit with Gordon and excitedly told Zack about it.

He smiled and asked, "Do you think she will want to see him?" He watched as her face clouded with concern.

"Oh my gosh. I hope so. I didn't even think about the fact she might not. Oh, no. Did I mess up?"

Zack took her hand. "I think what you did is a very nice thing, and I think there is a good chance she will want to see him, but don't be too disappointed if she doesn't."

Jen nodded. She was already committed to talking with Ingrid. She would call her in the morning. "Please, God, I hope I did the right thing."

Zack took her back to her car at the store. He got out and opened her door and walked her to her car. "It is going to be OK, Jen. Paulie is safe, and Gordon and Ingrid have their own Cupid." He reached down, cupped her face in his hands, and leaned down to give her a kiss of assurance. It quickly turned to a much deeper kiss, and when he pulled away, he saw her begin to blush. That was sweet. "Well, I'll see you tomorrow when we call John. I told him eight o'clock our time. Then I will take you out for coffee."

She nodded and got into her car. She was still feeling shaky when she got home. She really enjoyed those kisses. She fell asleep touching her lips and smiling.

CHAPTER 40

Paulie

Paulie was terrified. First, those men were going to come after him, and now he was in the car going to a safe house. The man beside him was very tall—taller than Zack. He had dark hair and a mustache. He seemed to be angry. He said he was Special Agent Joseph but that Paulie could call him Joe. Paulie decided he would just call him Agent Joe.

He shrank back into the seat as far as he could. He didn't want to make Agent Joe any angrier.

After ten minutes of silence, Agent Joe finally spoke. "Paulie, right?"

Paulie nodded.

"I know this can seem very scary for you, and I am sorry. I will be with you, and Gwen, who is a sheriff's deputy, will be at the safe house when we get there. I am from the FBI and helping because Zack is the only Homeland agent in this area. Tonight, two other agents will arrive. They will be with you all the time. We want to make it as easy as possible for you. I don't know what is happening or why you are in protective custody, but we will take care of you and keep you safe."

Paulie nodded. Maybe Agent Joe wasn't as angry as he thought.

They rode in silence for a while, then turned down a street.

"Are we in Kalispell?"

Agent Joe nodded. "We are going to be driving around for a while to make sure we are not being followed. I hope you don't get too confused."

After another twenty minutes, they pulled up to a small two-story house. Paulie noticed it was yellow and green. That was a weird mixture. All the lights were on.

Paulie started to get out of the car, but Agent Joe put out his hand. Let me check it out first. He got out of the car and came around to Paulie's side. He looked in all directions. When he got to Paulie's door, he opened it and said, "I want you to move quickly to the house. I will bring your things in after you."

Paulie moved toward the house as the door opened. A woman about forty years old was holding the door and ushered him in before quickly closing the door. She introduced herself as Deputy Gwen. Agent Joe went back to the car and brought in Paulie's luggage.

Paulie looked around and then followed Agent Joe to one of the bedrooms. There appeared to be two small bedrooms and an open kitchen, dining, and living room.

"There are two bedrooms upstairs, but we won't be using them," Agent Joe told him.

"I have pizza ready to eat anytime you are ready. I figured you haven't eaten."

As they ate, no one spoke. Paulie got up, took his dishes to the kitchen, and put them in the dishwasher. "Thank you, Deputy Gwen, for dinner. I think I will go to my room now."

For the next couple hours, Paulie worked on his computer and then lay down. He must have fallen asleep because he woke with a start when he heard someone at the door.

He went out into the living room and saw that two new people had arrived. One was a woman about twenty-four years old. She was blonde and petite. He noticed the gun she wore in a holster at her side. The other was a man who seemed to fill the doorway. He was shorter than Officer Joe but seemed to be almost square.

Both smiled at him as they introduced themselves.

"Hi. I am Kelly, and this is Tom. We are from the Seattle Homeland Security Office and will be staying with you for a while." She put out her hand, and while Paulie didn't like to touch, he put his hand out and let her shake it. Then Tom shook his hand.

"If you guys are set, I think I will go ahead and leave," Gwen said.

"Do you want me to hang around while you get settled?" Special Agent Joe asked.

Tom nodded at Gwen and turned to Officer Joe. "If you are up for staying for a few minutes and filling us in with what is going on and letting us get settled, I would appreciate it."

Gwen left, and Joe sat down. Kelly and Tom took their luggage into the second bedroom and came back and sat down.

"Paulie, how are you doing? Is there anything you need?" Kelly asked.

"Well, I forgot to have Jen pick up my deodorant and shampoo. I use only Degree no-scent deodorant and Dove shampoo."

Kelly smiled. "I think we can arrange that."

Joe said. "I can pick those up. Walmart is close. I'll pick them up when I leave and drop them off."

"Thank you. I am sorry I am trouble …" Paulie started to say.

"It's OK, Paulie. We know this is difficult. It's hard when you leave your home in a hurry. I understand that you weren't even allowed to go back. It's all good."

Joe filled them in on what he knew. They visited for a while, and then he left, promising to return shortly with Paulie's things.

Tom got up, went to the refrigerator, and pulled out the leftover pizza. "Do you want some, Kelly?" She nodded.

As he was heating up the food and they ate, they talked with Paulie. He was surprised how easy it was to talk with them and that they seemed interested in him.

A few minutes later, they heard a car pull up. Tom looked at the window and quickly turned around. "Get Paulie out of here *now*!"

Kelly grabbed Paulie's hand and pulled him through the back door. At the same time, she pulled out her phone and called 911. "Officer needs assistance." She rattled off the address and continued to pull Paulie along.

After running three blocks, she pulled Paulie behind a hedge. "I'm going to need to pull up a map and find out where we are." They heard shots. Paulie started to move toward the house. "No, you need to stay safe."

"I know where we are. I watched as Officer Joe drove me here. In two blocks, there is a service station—uh, Shell, I think. In that direction is a mall with a movie theater and restaurant. I think it said Shirley's."

"Have you been here before?"

"No, I just remember things."

"Let's go to Shirley's." As they quickly walked in the direction Paulie had indicated, Kelly pulled out her phone and called Zack. She outlined what had happened.

They arrived at the restaurant, went in, and sat down.

"Zack will meet us in a few minutes."

Kelly ordered coffee, and Paulie ordered a piece of cherry pie, heated and with ice cream. By the time Paulie finished his pie, Zack walked in the door. Paulie asked where Jen was. He insisted he needed her.

Zack called Jen and quickly explained where they were and the sketchy details of what he knew. She told him she would be there in twenty minutes.

As he was finishing the phone call, Joe and Tom walked in.

Each of them told their story. When they got to the part where Paulie and Kelly left, Tom picked up his story. "I saw a car arrive, and when the door opened, it showed two men. That's when I told Kelly to get Paulie out. I made sure the door was locked and pulled back into the room. They broke the door and came in. I yelled, 'Stop!' and the first one shot at me. I returned fire."

Joe picked up the story. "I heard the officer-down call as I was pulling up to the house. I saw the men enter and came up behind them. I heard Tom's shot as I was identifying myself. The second one turned and aimed his gun, and I shot him. Both men are dead. The police arrived. I gave them the story and told them we had to go but would come in later and give our statements. They weren't happy, but we didn't give them a choice."

"Only John, each of you, and the deputy knew where we were taking Paulie."

"The deputy got out of there pretty fast after we arrived. Do you think she called someone? Or had someone somehow followed one of us?"

"My call is the deputy. I drove around for twenty minutes to make sure no one followed us when I took Paulie to the safe house. Other than the deputy, I am the only one who knew your agents were arriving tonight."

Zack nodded. First, he called John and gave him a rundown of the events of the night. John said he would arrange another safe house and would call him back. Next, he called his friend Justin. He was a state trooper. Zack gave him a brief outline and asked him to pick up the deputy, Gwen. "I don't trust anyone in the sheriff's department right now. If you bring her to Whitefish, we can question her there and hopefully keep it under wraps for a while."

When Jen arrived, she practically flew into the restaurant. First, she grabbed Paulie and hugged him even though he squirmed. She reached over and touched Zack's shoulder.

Zack's phone rang. It was John. He gave him the address of the new safe house. He told him two other agents from Seattle would be arriving tomorrow morning. He informed him he had called the sheriff and told him Joe and Tom would come in the next morning to give their statements.

Zack introduced everyone and filled them in on the plan. Joe, Kelly, and Tom would take him to the new safe house, and all three would stay the night. After the new agents arrived, Tom and Joe would go in and make their statements, then pick up the rental car and Paulie's things and their luggage, which were still at the house.

As they were beginning to leave, Jen mentioned the bug in her house and wondered if there was any way they might put a tracking device on the rental car. They all nodded, and Tom said he would make sure to check it out when he picked up the car.

Zack would ride back with Jen to Whitefish, and she could drop him off at the police department, where he would hopefully question Gwen. They decided Kelly and Joe would drive in Joe's car, and Tom would follow and make sure no one was following them.

CHAPTER 41

Zack

Zack ran his fingers through his hair. He was exhausted and was jittery from all the coffee he had consumed. The only good thought he had was about the tight hug and kiss that Jen had given him when she dropped him off.

Justin had found Gwen and brought her in. Another state trooper had stopped by the police department in Kalispell and picked up the phones of the two men who had attacked that were in evidence.

The phones did not have a password, so they had opened them. Sure enough, when they compared Gwen's phone to theirs, they found Gwen had called one of them minutes after she left the safe house. When Zack questioned her, she was tearful and said, "They said they just wanted to talk to him, that no one would get hurt."

Zack shook his head. "What did you think would happen then?"

She just put her head down. She refused to give up the names of anyone else she was working with.

He had her put in the jail cell and decided there was nothing else he could do. He thanked Justin and the other trooper for their help. He and Justin agreed they needed to get together when this was all over. He went home, hoping he could get a couple hours of sleep.

Zack's alarm went off at seven. He had fallen into bed with his clothes on at five. It had been a short night. He thought of Jen and smiled. He knew he should be concentrating on the job, but something about that woman had captivated him. She was sweet and smart and kind, and, well, she was certainly something else.

He made a quick call to see how she was doing and to confirm they were still going to talk with John. The time had been moved to nine o'clock. She would go to his office.

He sat down, read his Bible, and then prayed. He prayed Paulie would remain safe and not have too much difficulty staying at the safe house. He prayed for the job, and he prayed for Jen, and he prayed that God would lead his heart where it needed to be. He knew he didn't want to ask God for Jen, in case He said no. He also he knew he needed God's blessing. He had pursued relationships before without caring what God wanted, and they had not turned out well.

He arrived at the office at 7:45 and paced. They needed to do this job right. They needed to stop these people, and he and Jen needed to do the relationship right, if they were going to have one.

When she walked in the door, he looked up and noticed she blushed. So sweet. He wanted to take her in his arms right then and there but held himself back. This job was important; they needed to take care of that first.

He called John and put the phone on speaker. For over an hour, they discussed the incidents of the night before and progress they had made with Gwen's arrest and tracking the vehicles. They discussed the plan. They all knew they needed to do this as soon as they could to prevent more victims from being hurt, but they also knew they needed to do this right if they were going to shut down the operation.

CHAPTER 42

Jen

Jen was invigorated with the job she was doing. She had prayed this morning, thanking God for watching out for Paulie and the others. She prayed for guidance for the investigation as well as her and Zack's relationship. She felt good about the conversation with John and that they were on the right track. After coffee, Zack had walked her to her car and touched her elbow and then wrapped her in a hug. Then he lifted her face for a kiss. Was she ready for this?

She went home and called Paulie. He seemed to be doing well for all he had been through. She compiled some of the data they were receiving. She added some filters. She called Ingrid and asked if she could drop by in the afternoon. Then she went into the office.

Fortunately, there was little to do at the office, so she quickly took care of what was necessary. Then she sat and thought about her life, Zack, and her work. She liked writing the algorithms and working with Zack. She had also enjoyed looking for Gordon. She always felt more alive when she was investigating and doing research. She felt she had a real gift for it. How could she find a job that would give her those kinds of opportunities and the freedom to work on her own?

CHAPTER 43

Ingrid

At two o'clock, she headed over to Ingrid's house. When she arrived, Ingrid invited her to the patio. She served lemonade and set a plate of freshly baked cookies. Jen took warm chocolate chip cookie, then took a deep breath and said, "Um, you remember when you told me your story, and you mentioned Gordon? Well, I got curious about him and decided to do some investigating, and I found him, and, well, he lives in Bigfork, and I went to see him, and he wants to see you."

Ingrid just stared at her. Jen took a breath. "I'm sorry if I shouldn't have. I just wanted to see you happy. You are so kind to so many. I wanted to do something for you, but if I shouldn't have, I am …"

Ingrid put up her hand to stop Jen. "I am just in shock and not sure how I feel. I wasn't sure if he would even remember me."

"Oh, he remembered you. He said you were his first true love, and, well, I guess I should let him tell you—that is, if you want to meet him."

Ingrid thought for a minute and nodded. “I think I would like to do that.”

They talked about how to make it the most comfortable and decided it might be best to meet in a neutral place but not in public. Jen suggested her house. Ingrid liked that idea.

“It is Thursday, so what if I see if he is willing to come over on Saturday? That way, you don’t have to wait too long, so you both don’t get too nervous and back out.” Jen smiled. “I will have a little lunch for you, and you can sit on my patio and visit. If you get uncomfortable or want to leave, you can. How does that sound?”

Ingrid smiled. “That sounds lovely.”

Jen agreed to let her know more details once she had talked with Gordon.

As Jen drove home, she found herself smiling and humming. She parked, let CD out of the car, and went in the house. She gave CD water and his food and then went out onto the patio. She called Gordon’s number, and he answered on the first ring.

“What did she say? Is she willing to meet?”

Jen smiled and told him about the plan to meet on Saturday if he was willing to do that. He enthusiastically said yes. She promised to text him the time and her address. When she hung up, she texted him the information and then called Ingrid. She answered on the first ring as well. Jen told her the plan was a go and she would see her on Saturday.

After making the calls, she went into her office and checked the computer for results. It appeared that there was a pattern of where the cars traveled and where they stopped. She was able to track nine of the original twelve vehicles Paulie had given them. She had found seventeen other vehicles that were registered to the same shell company. She was excited; they appeared to be getting closer.

She called Zack, and he answered on the first ring. It was her day for people to enthusiastically answer her calls.

She explained the results she was seeing and then told him about Ingrid and Gordon. She could hear the smile in his voice. She invited him over for tacos, and he accepted. It was a good day.

Next, she called Paulie, and he answered on the third ring. *Oh well, can't win them all.*

Paulie talked about the agent, Kelly, and told Jen how he had explained his work to her. She told him she liked to make things from kits and was always frustrated when something came and the directions weren't clear. Paulie sounded pleased. He told her he was sure he would be OK there until this was all over. Jen had noticed how easily Kelly had talked with Paulie the night before and how she did not seem put off by his quirkiness.

CHAPTER 44

Zack

Zack ran his hands through his hair in frustration. This was such a huge undertaking. With the vehicles Paulie had told them about and the others they determined were owned by the same company, they were all over the country. Jen had found a pattern; she had even been able to determine approximate times of drop-offs and pick-ups. She found some vehicles that appeared to be going back and forth across the border. They had to decide when and where the best places would be to take them down. It needed to be when they were exchanging so they could catch as many of the players as possible. They were going to use local law enforcement, but that would increase the chances of a leak, especially after the problem with Gwen last night. They decided to use the FBI and Homeland Security as much as possible and then call local enforcement in at the last minute. That way, if there were any local authorities who were in on it, they would not have a chance to warn them. Zack hoped that they could take down a large number of them at once. This would increase their chances of flipping some of the players and make the odds better of getting the major players. He was hoping they could stop these evil people.

It appeared the days they transported the most were Sunday and Monday. This was probably because that was when the traffic crossing the borders was at its highest, and vehicles were less likely to be checked. Zack and John had agreed that they would shoot for two weeks from Sunday to begin the sting. Until then, there was a lot to do. He was glad Jen had invited him to her house to see how Gordon and Ingrid got along. He knew Jen was hoping for a happy ending, and he liked the idea that love could last through the years, but if it didn't go well, he wanted to be there with her.

CHAPTER 45

Jen

Jen checked one more time to see that everything was in place. Ice, tea, lemonade, glasses, and chicken salad croissant sandwiches were already set up on the patio. She had talked with Ingrid and Gordon that morning. They both seemed a little nervous but excited. She had assured them that she would be there with a friend. She would stay out of the way once they met, unless either one of them needed something or wanted her around.

Zack showed up first with a bouquet of flowers. "Romance needs flowers," he announced. CD bounced around, waiting for Zack's attention.

"For them or for me?" She smiled. "CD, calm down. He acts like a puppy when you are around."

He gave her the crooked grin, then reached over and gave her a kiss. It started as just a little kiss and then began to take on a life of its own. The doorbell rang. They each pulled back, and Jen noticed Zack looked a little flush. She smiled; this was becoming a habit, a nice one.

When she answered the door, she found Ingrid standing there, wringing her hands. She greeted her and invited her in. CD immediately went up to her and sat. Ingrid greeted CD with a nervous pat, not rubbing his neck as she usually did.

"Are you OK, Ingrid?"

"Well, I am not sure about this. I was a young, pretty girl when I knew him. Today, I am just an old, wrinkled lady."

Before Jen could respond and encourage her, the doorbell rang again. "Why don't you let Zack take you out to the patio and pour you a glass of tea while I get the door." Ingrid nodded, and Zack escorted her outside.

Jen opened the door to a smiling Gordon. He had two bouquets of flowers in his hand. He gave her one. "From your garden?" He nodded.

CD came back from the patio, where he had followed Ingrid and Zack, and sat down next to Gordon. "Well, who is this handsome dog?" Gordon kneeled and petted him. When he stood, he looked at her a little anxiously. "I couldn't sleep all night. I am so excited to see her again."

Jen motioned for him to come in and showed him out onto the patio. Ingrid had her back to them; she was admiring the rock flower garden Jen was working on. Or at least she was pretending to. When she turned, she let out her breath and saw Gordon open his arm. "Ingrid, I would know those beautiful eyes anywhere. You are so beautiful."

Ingrid's face lit up, and she walked right into his arms. When they pulled apart, he handed Ingrid the second bouquet. Jen offered them iced tea or lemonade, but they did not seem to hear her. She left the pitchers there and motioned for Zack to follow her inside.

For the next two hours, Zack and Jen sat in the family room and played gin rummy to pass the time. They talked about the plans for the takedown the following Sunday. Jen encouraged him to talk about his mother and their recent visit to keep him from stressing. He told her his mother wanted to meet her.

"Do you want me to meet her?"

"Absolutely. I want the two women of my life to meet and get to know each other. I know she will love you like I do." Jen started; had he said *love*? She started to ask him when Ingrid stuck her head in and asked for some more napkins. Jen got up and gave her some.

Zack mentioned that Gordon and Ingrid were talking like a couple lovestruck teenagers. They laughed. Jen felt her heart swell. *Thank you, God, that they have this chance to get reacquainted.*

Later, she went out to check on them, and they looked up, startled, like they had forgotten where they were and that anyone was around.

"Jen, thank you, sweet girl, for this gift. It feels like it was just yesterday that we were walking home from piano practice," Gordon said. Jen saw Ingrid nodding and smiling and a tear trailing down her face.

They both stood and arranged to have lunch the next day, then left together hand in hand.

"Well done, Ms. Matchmaker."

Jen smiled. "I think God might have been the matchmaker. I just helped orchestrate it. I have a couple heavy rocks and things I could really use some extra muscle for. Are you interested?"

"Interested in being your muscle? Anytime, ma'am."

Jen took him to the side of the house where several large rocks were on a cart. "I need these taken to the rock garden and then help unloading and placing them." He nodded and started pulling the cart. Together they worked until the light in the sky started to fade. They placed the last rock, took off their gloves, and headed for the patio. Jen went in the house and brought out two large glasses of ice water. They toasted to a successful afternoon.

Zack stayed for dinner—leftovers from the lunch for Ingrid and Gordon.

They decided thar after church the next day, they would spend time taking the data she had gathered and identifying as many locations as they could. He told her he would bring lunch and the map, and they could work.

She walked him to the door. Zack turned to go. He was halfway down the walk and then quickly came back, grabbed her, and kissed her, a kiss that curled her toes. "To make sure you will be thinking about me." He turned and quickly left.

Oh, yeah, she would definitely be thinking of him.

That night, as she was falling asleep, she again heard the perimeter warning go off. She got up, turned on the lights, and checked. She did not see anyone on the cameras, so she went back to bed.

CHAPTER 46

Jen

Jen and Zack had worked for four hours mapping out the data she had collected. They were able to determine a route that nineteen of the vehicles appeared to take. With the time lapses between cameras catching the cars entering and leaving cities, they were able to determine seventeen cities where transfers appeared to be made. They had marked each one on a map.

Zack sighed, stood, and stretched. "I think my brain is mush, and I need a break."

Jen stood and turned just as he moved to the door, bringing them face-to-face. Jen saw the desire in his eyes as he bent down to kiss her. The kiss became more urgent. She felt the world begin to spin. She moved her fingers to his hair. She felt like she was drowning. He moved her so her back was against the wall. And then he bumped a glass, and it fell to the floor and broke. Jen hit the floor.

When she realized what she had done, she stood up. "I am so sorry. Sometimes noises like that—well, I just react."

Zack nodded. "I need to go. I will talk with you tomorrow." With that, he turned around and left.

Jen just stood there. It happened again. Her reaction embarrassed him, and he didn't want to be around her. She just stood there, not even aware that the tears were streaming down her face.

The rest of the afternoon, she went about small chores as if on automatic. She felt like a ton of weight was on her chest.

She lay in bed, struggling to find sleep. "God, I don't understand why You brought him into my life only to take him away. Please help me get through this."

CHAPTER 47

Zack

Zack couldn't believe he had left that way when he realized that the kiss had moved beyond what it should have. He had come too close to crossing the line. He had promised God that he if he entered another relationship, he would be honorable to the woman and pleasing to God. He would not let his physical desires take over. Yet he had. He had wanted to continue with Jen; he wanted to make love to her and would have had the glass not dropped.

He drove around and found himself in Polson at his mother's. He parked and went in. His mother looked up when he walked in, and the smile that came to her left as suddenly. She saw he was in pain.

Zack explained how he had promised God to be responsible with his emotions. He had asked God to hold them in check so he acted like a child of God. Then he told his mother what had happed with Jen. He told her how the kiss had deepened, how he had wanted to make love to her, and if the glass had not fallen, how he would have continued.

His mother smiled. "Oh, sweet boy. I am so proud of you. Please understand that God put those feelings and desires in you. If you read the Song of Solomon, you understand the longing that came with attraction and love. It's natural that this happened. When you care about someone, maybe love them," she said, her eyes questioning, "those emotions and desires are even stronger. Just because you turned your life over to God does not mean He takes those desires away. The fact that in the past you have acted on those feelings and desires without regard for the consequences makes it more difficult to stop. God does not ask us not to act on those desires because He wants to set rules. He gave us those directions because He wants us to have more than just the physical connection. He wants us to love and commit so we can demonstrate that love in the physical action. Our strong sexual desire is to help move us in that direction. If we only go with the sexual desire, however, it will soon burn out, and then we are left with emptiness. When we honor God and the other person by waiting, He will bless the relationship even more. Don't you see? The glass falling was not just an accident."

Zack nodded. "I don't deserve her, Mom. I messed up so much in the past. I don't deserve for her to love me."

"That is where there is grace. God knows your heart. Remember, when we confess our sins and turn from our ways, God removes that sin, and to Him, it is no longer there. We wake up each morning with a clean slate. I am concerned about how you left Jen. Don't you think maybe you need to explain it to her?"

His mother fixed him her famous tomato soup and grilled cheese sandwich, and they visited for several hours.

It was late by the time he headed home. He would go see Jen in the morning and explain.

CHAPTER 48

Jen

When the doorbell rang at seven the next morning, Jen was surprised that she had been feeling so sad she had not even heard the warning go off.

She opened the door, and Zack stood there. She didn't know what to do.

"Would you take a walk with me?"

She nodded. "I need to put my shoes on."

After putting on her shoes, she walked slowly to the door. She was dreading this conversation.

They walked in silence for several minutes. Jen started, "It really is OK. I know how embarrassing it is when someone reacts like that. I am glad it wasn't in public. It would have been more embarrassing for you."

He stopped, and she saw the confused look on his face.

"You know, when I just dropped to the floor when the glass fell."

He saw the hurt in her eyes, and it dawned on him what she was saying. Shaking his head, he responded, "Jen, I am so sorry. That is not why I left."

Now he saw the confused look on her face. "Jen, I have had a number of relationships. In the past, if I desired someone, then I just went ahead, and we had sex. This would last for as long as the other person and I were interested, and then it would end. When I came to God, I realized the sexual relationship between a man and woman was much more than self-gratification. It was meant to be special and exclusive. I realized I had used these women, even though I had cared about them, but for my own desires. I made a promise to God that I would not do that. Yesterday, when I kissed you, I wanted you. I wanted to make love to you, and that was the only thought in my head. The only thing that stopped me from going further was the glass falling. The sound brought me back to reality and made me realize what I was doing. I needed to get out of there and sort it out."

He took a breath. "I went and saw my mom. She helped me see that it was OK to desire you and want you like that because I am starting to really care about you. I want to apologize that I was ready to push it further."

Jen reached up and touched his face. "I was part of that kiss, too, remember. I was allowing it to move further than it should have. Thank you for sharing this with me. I am really starting to care about you too. Let's try to figure this out together."

She saw relief in his eyes as he nodded. Then he bent and kissed her on her forehead. "Thanks for understanding."

They returned home, and Jen fixed breakfast. They decided to finish the project of mapping the locations. As he left, he bent down and kissed her, a hopeful kiss.

CHAPTER 49

Holly

Holly was four years old. She was alone and scared. A woman had come to her day care. They were outside playing. Holly was playing by herself. The woman had rushed up to her and told her that her mother had been hurt and was in the hospital, and Holly had to come with her. The woman had grabbed her hand and dragged her into a car. When she looked out the window of the car, she saw Mrs. Taylor running after them. They drove for a few minutes, and then the woman and a man picked her up and put her in a van.

Holly was crying, asking for her mother.

"Shut up." The woman slapped her.

Holly made herself as small as she could and moved to a corner in the van. She fell asleep crying. She woke when the woman jerked on her and told her to come with her.

They took her into a room with three other little girls. Holly looked around. It looked like a room they had stayed in when they went to visit Disneyland. It had a bed and television. It wasn't as nice as that room, and it smelled a little funny.

The other girls were crying and about her age. They looked like they might go to a school like she did. Her mom called it preschool. Holly just called it school.

The woman and another woman came into the room. They made them dress in frilly dresses, like the ones Holly wore to church. They took pictures and made them change out of the pretty dresses. Then they left. Holly tried to open the door, but it was locked.

Later, the second woman came back and brought them hamburgers from McDonald's. She was nicer than the other woman. She gave them each an orange juice. Holly remembered feeling kind of funny after that. Then she fell asleep.

In the morning, they brought them another hamburger and turned on the television to cartoons. Holly was scared. She just wanted to go home.

Holly was tired of hamburgers. Her mom said it wasn't good to eat at McDonald's very often.

The women told them that the next day they were going on a trip. Then gave them more orange juice. Holly remembered feeling funny again. Then she fell asleep.

CHAPTER 50

Cara

They stopped fighting finally. Mrs. Jenson had been more hurtful than usual. She had yelled more and pinched Cara often. She seemed to find fault in everything Cara did.

He had come in last night. He had hurt her. He no longer treated her with any gentleness. He sneered at her and told her she would soon be gone. They were going to come and get her tomorrow. She should be glad he had shown her all the ropes. She was prepared to be a working girl.

After he left, Cara lay in bed crying. She understood what he meant. She knew he had sold her so she could be used as a prostitute.

"God, are You there? Can You help me?" Then she fell into a fitful sleep.

They woke her early and gave her a sack for her few belonging. Two men came to the door. They tied her hands. She did not look back. One man opened the door to a van. She started to get in and then backed up. It smelled like someone had been sick in it. She started to struggle, and one of the men slapped her and shoved her into the van. She landed on her shoulder. He slammed the door.

"Please, God, help me. Please, God, help the girl they are bringing here."

CHAPTER 51

Zack

Sleep had been elusive for Zack; he went over and over in his mind how the operation was to go down and racked his brain to see if he had forgotten anything. The past week, they had gone over the details of the operation at least twenty times. He tried to think of something else, and inevitably, his thoughts went to Jen. They had hiked for a couple hours yesterday to work off the tension. She had shown him some new trails. They were easily matched and appeared to enjoy the same things. Zack had identified several plants, and they had discussed her love for gardening. They had dinner last night. Before he left, Jen had prayed for the safety of everyone involved in the operation. Zack told her that Kelly would be dropping off Paulie the next afternoon. The kiss goodbye had been sweet. Jen had held on to him. "Please be safe," she had whispered.

She had become such an important part of his life. She was all the things he wanted in a woman, and when he thought of her not being in his life, he felt a pain in his chest. When he thought of the kisses, he knew he wanted to have more. With Jen, the desire was certainly there, but there was so much more: a desire to protect, a desire to make her smile, a desire to work with her, side by side, a desire to know her better. "Lord, help me to be a man worthy of her."

At five o'clock in the morning, he got up, showered, dressed, and made coffee.

He probably should not have had an entire pot of coffee. His nerves felt a little jangly. He was glad his partner was Jacob. They had worked together before, and he knew Jacob was a believer. When Jacob got into the car, Zack asked if he could pray for them. Jacob agreed, let Zack pray, and then added a couple things before saying amen. Zack felt calmer and was ready to get this over with.

Agents were at seventeen different locations they had determined were exchange points. The earliest would be in Denver at about seven o'clock. Zack was overseeing the operation and gave the go-ahead. He and Jacob sat in the parking lot near Paulie's house. At nine thirty, two vans pulled into the parking lot, side by side. The drivers got out. Zack and Jacob pulled into a parking space next to them and casually got out. As they neared the drivers Zack yelled, "Homeland Security, put up your hands." Two Montana state troopers pulled up next to them with their guns drawn. Zack was next to the passenger in the van and saw him start to move.

Zack pointed his gun at him. "I wouldn't do that if I were you." The man raised his hands and got out of the van. As Zack cuffed him, one of the troopers opened the back of the second van.

Inside was a man with his gun pointed at a little girl; she looked to be only three or four years old.

"I will hurt her if you come any closer."

The two troopers and Zack pointed their guns at the man. "There is no need to hurt anyone. Let's just talk."

"I'm not going to talk; you are going to back up and close the door. I am going to get in and drive away, or the little girl gets hurt."

Out of the corner of his eye, Zack saw Jacob. The door had been left open when they pulled the man out. Jacob was slipping into the van.

Zack told the troopers to back up.

Zack nodded. He kept talking as the man moved toward the front of the van. When he had almost reached the front seat, he saw Jacob reach around and grabbed the man's arm that was holding the gun and put a cuff on him. With his other hand, he pointed at the man's head with his gun.

"Now let the little girl go."

The man growled but let the little girl go.

Zack nodded at the little girl and held his arms out for her. She launched herself at him.

The troopers took the four men and put them in the cars to transport them. Zack and Jacob rounded up the two passengers from the other car. Both appeared to be in their preteens.

Zack and Jacob transported the victims back to the station. The little girl was named Holly. They determined she had been kidnapped two days before from her preschool in Seeley Lake. They contacted her parents, who were soon on their way to pick her up.

It appeared the other two girls had been kidnapped several years earlier. They gave their names as Cara and Jessica. Zack's boss had people working on their identities and contacting their families.

Zack overheard Cara telling Jessica, "I prayed and prayed God would help me, and He finally did. He does love me." Jessica just cried.

Zack sent up a quick prayer of thanks.

CHAPTER 52

Jen

When she woke, she had a sense of dread. Maybe it was from lack of sleep, or maybe it was knowing what was about to happen and being worried things could go wrong. She just couldn't shake it. "Father, I know that You are there, and You are protecting Zack and the others. I know You hate evil. Please let this operation go smoothly so that arrests can be made and the trafficking by these people can be stopped."

She went to church and prayed throughout the service. She heard little of the music or the sermon, but she felt a sense of peace as she left. She saw Ingrid and Gordon sitting side by side. She went over and greeted them. They were all smiles and looked like lovesick teenagers. It was good.

When she got home, she changed into yoga pants and a top and took CD for a walk. When they returned from the walk, it was twelve forty, so she decided to leave the door open and the screen door shut. Paulie would be there soon, and if he saw the door open, he would just go in.

She walked out to the patio and looked at the rock garden. She needed to pick up some flowers for it. She heard the warning go off that someone was outside, so she turned and went into the kitchen. "I'm out here, Paulie. I …"

There was a man just inside the door, holding a gun. He had a wild look in his eye.

"Who are you, and what are you doing?"

"You—you ruined Tim's life. He's dead because of you. You put him in jail, and he killed himself. That is on you."

Jen took a breath. "I'm sorry, please tell me who you are. I don't understand."

The man was waving the gun around wildly. "You, you killed him."

Jen remembered Tim. He had been one of the officers she had investigated. He had been taking money from ISIS and had given them locations of some of the teams. Twenty men had died because of him.

"Please, you don't understand. Tim got people killed—"

"No, he would not do that." He raised the gun just as CD lunged for him. Jen heard the shot, felt the pain in her shoulder, and everything turned black.

CHAPTER 53

Paulie

Kelly was pulling into Jen's driveway to drop Paulie off when she heard a gunshot. She quickly put the car into park and dove out. As she pulled out her gun, she yelled to Paulie, "Stay back! Don't go in!" but it was too late. Paulie rushed inside.

She bolted in after him and almost ran him down. On the floor was a man with a gun just inches from his hand and a large dog with his mouth around the man's throat. The man had soiled himself and was whimpering. She grabbed at Paulie to pull him back, but instead he moved forward. "It's OK, CD. You did good." The dog let go of the man's throat and immediately moved around the counter and started whining. Paulie saw Jen lying on the floor, blood all around.

Kelly quickly moved to kick the man's gun out of the way and pulled out her cuffs to cuff him. She took out her cell phone, identified herself, and asked for an ambulance and backup.

Paulie was on his knees, crying. "Jen, Jen, you have to wake up.

You have to be OK, Jen." He started to shake her. Kelly put her hand on Paulie's shoulder.

"Paulie, careful. The ambulance is on the way. Could you move out of the way so I can try to get the bleeding stopped?" As she said it, there was a deep growl from the dog standing guard. Kelly backed up slowly and raised her hands.

Paulie went over and wrapped his arms around the dog. "It's OK, CD. She is a friend. She will help us." The dog seemed to understand and lay down next to the woman. He watched the deputy. Kelly knew the dog would spring at her in a second if he thought she was hurting the woman.

"Paulie, I have the ambulance coming. Could you take the dog into the other room so they can work?"

He nodded, got up, and called CD. He had to call him several times before the dog followed him. They went into the room, and he shut the door. The dog started howling a heartbreaking sound. Kelly fought the tears. That dog really loved this woman.

Behind the door, Paulie was crying and holding CD, trying to comfort him. He reached in his pocket and got his phone. He had to call Zack; he had to let him know. He pushed the speed dial number and waited. It went to voice mail. He tried again and again.

The ambulance arrived, and they quickly prepared Jen for transport. Kelly knocked on the door and told Paulie what was happening. She asked if he wanted a ride to the hospital or to stay with the dog. He opened the door, and the dog rushed out and went looking for his master. Paulie seemed to be struggling with what to do.

"Why don't you stay with the dog for now and calm him down. I am going to follow the ambulance. I will call you or come get you as soon as I know what is going on." Paulie nodded.

Paulie sat in the room crying as CD howled. He dialed Zack again.

CHAPTER 54

Zack

Zack walked down the hall of the police station and grabbed some coffee. He probably didn't need it but figured it was going to be a long day. Of the seventeen locations, they had been able to make arrests at sixteen of them. There had been one firefight, and thankfully no victims had been hurt. One of the kidnappers had been killed, and another was injured and in surgery. One of the agents had been injured but was already treated and released. He took off his hat and brushed his fingers through his hair. The adrenaline had worn off. He noticed his phone vibrating. He looked at the caller ID and saw that Paulie had called nineteen times. He ignored it for the moment and called his supervisor for a report.

"Zack, we were able to pick up twenty-seven vehicles and rescue thirty-seven people. Some of their vehicles apparently didn't make it to the rendezvous point before we began the arrests. You did a good job coordinating this. We will take them to various lockups, question them, and see what more we can find out."

Zack's phone vibrated again, and this time he saw a text that said "SOS." He explained it to his supervisor and called Paulie. Paulie answered the phone on the first ring. Zack could hear him crying and CD howling in the background.

"Paulie, take a breath. What is it?"

"Jen, she was shot, and CD saved her, and she had to go to the hospital, and CD is upset, and …"

As Zack listened, he felt his stomach plummet. Jen was hurt—shot. What was going on? Was she OK? "OK, Paulie, start over and tell me what happened." Paulie explained how they heard a shot when he arrived, and then he found CD holding the man and Jen on the floor with lots of blood and unconscious.

"I need to get to Jen, but I don't want CD alone."

Zack took a deep breath. "Where are you, Paulie?" Paulie told him he was at Jen's with CD. "I am coming right now; I will pick you up, and we will go to the hospital. Did they say which one? Are they taking her to Kalispell Regional?"

"I think so." The sobs were starting to slow, but the howling continued.

CHAPTER 55

Zack and Paulie and CD

Zack quickly informed Jacob about what had happened. Jacob assured him he could handle things. Tom had come to the station when Kelly left to drop Paulie off. He could help. Zack contacted John. John confirmed they could handle it and he should go. Zack agreed to check in later to give them an update and to check on the operation.

Zack put the siren on the dash and raced to Jen's house. On the way, he contacted the local police and confirmed where they had taken her. He sent up a desperate prayer for her to be OK. He knew he had fallen in love with her. The thought of Jen not being in his life gripped him like a vice grip. He didn't want to lose her. As he pulled in, he saw Paulie racing from the house. He grabbed Paulie and hugged him, and he didn't seem to mind. He asked where CD was, and Paulie walked him into the house. The dog looked terrible. He lay on the floor whimpering and dejected. Zack remembered that CD had stayed at his first partner's side until they took him away. CD was reliving his worst nightmare.

"Come on, boy, we are going to show you she is OK." With another quick prayer, he pleaded for Jen to be OK.

Paulie got into the car with CD after grabbing his leash. Zack drove quickly, with the lights and siren blaring all the way to the hospital. Paulie told him again how they had heard the shot and went in and found CD with his mouth around the man's neck and Jen on the floor, with all the blood.

When they got to the hospital, they ran toward the door. The hospital guard tried to stop them, but Zack showed his badge and told him the dog had just saved Jen's life (*Please let that be so*), and he allowed them in.

They were told Jen was still in surgery and where the waiting room was. Zack had put his badge on his belt, thinking it might make things go more smoothly. Security eyed the trio, but he pointed to the badge, and they showed him where the elevators were.

When they got off the elevators, they saw Kelly. She told them there had not been any news. Zack filled her in on the operation and how many they had arrested and the number of victims who were now safe.

While they waited, Zack called John. John assured him the interrogations were going well. Many of the ones they had questioned had already given up names of people higher up the chain. Several arrest warrants had been issued, and search warrants were being processed.

CHAPTER 56

Jen

They waited for what felt hours, CD occasionally whimpering. At first, they sat silently, and then Paulie began to tell Kelly and Zack how Jen had led him to God. He told them how she had held his hand as he confessed he needed a Savior and asked Jesus into his heart. He talked about how Jen had helped to make his life bearable in school when they were young, how she had never treated him like he was different. He talked about how much he had missed her those years she was away in the army. Tears ran down his face. "I don't want her to die. I want her here with us, with CD."

"Me, too, Paulie. Me too. It's in the doctors' and God's hands. We know Jen loves God and that whatever happens is His will." Zack felt a knife go through his stomach as he thought about her not making it. He noticed Kelly giving them a questioning look.

The doctor came through the doors. "Are you here for Jen Stander?" They nodded. "Are you family?"

Zack and Paulie jumped to their feet. He showed his badge and explained who he was and that she had no family there. He asked if her phone was with her belongings when she came in and found out it had been in her pocket. He asked that they get it to him so he could call her father.

"So," Zack said shakily, "is she OK?"

The doctor explained that the bullet had gone into the clavicle and lodged there. They had been able to remove it, and she was expected to make a full recovery. They asked if they could go see her. He said she still had not wakened, but when she did, he would arrange it. The doctor noticed the dog and started to tell them he could not be there.

"The dog saved her life and now needs to know she is OK. I'll take full responsibility, but he's going in." The doctor nodded, realizing it wouldn't help to argue.

"I'll have someone bring the phone, and someone will come out and get you when she wakes."

Zack thanked him.

In a few minutes, someone brought Jen's phone to them. Paulie was able to figure out which name was her father's. Zack made the call.

"Jen-girl, how are you, sweetheart?"

"Mr. Stander, my name is Zack Julian. I work for Homeland Security and am a friend of Jen's."

"She mentioned you when we talked. Is she OK?"

"Yes, she is OK. I am at the hospital now. She was shot, but we don't know the story yet. The doctor said she is expected to make a full recovery. I am here with Paulie and CD, and we will be going in to see her as soon as she is awake."

Zack heard her father let out a breath. "I had hoped we could meet under different circumstances. My girl thinks you are something special, and the fact that you are there with Paulie and CD tells me she is right. I will catch the next flight out and be there as soon as I can. Kalispell Regional, right?"

Zack asked if he needed a ride from the airport, and her father assured him he would arrange for a rental car and be there as soon as he could. Before he hung up, he said, "Take care of my girl. My phone will be off when I fly, but I will turn it on at each layover."

Zack asked if Paulie was hungry. It was 9:00 p.m., and they had been there for several hours. They couldn't take CD to the cafeteria because dogs weren't allowed, so Kelly offered to get them some sandwiches, chips, and drinks. Paulie sat quietly, stroking CD's head. The dog looked dejected but had stopped most of the whimpering. A detective came by to see if he could get a statement from Jen. Zack explained she was asleep, but he would let him know when she woke up.

They ate their sandwiches, and Zack called Jacob in Whitefish to see how things were at the jail. Jacob told Zack all the prisoners had been booked. As much as he wanted to be there to question them, he could not leave Jen right then. He contacted John and updated him on Jen. John said the interrogations continued to go well. Zack felt torn between staying with Jen and going back to the jail to interrogate the men in his custody. "Why don't you stay with your girl? Let's see how it goes, but we have things under control for now. You did a great job, and I think those guys can wait."

Zack thanked him and sighed in relief. As he turned to talk with Paulie, the nurse came and said they could go in. Jen looked pale and groggy, but as they walked into the room, CD let out a yelp and practically pulled Paulie over as he went to her bed. Jen opened her eyes, those beautiful eyes. She reached out to CD, and Paulie started talking.

"Jen, I was so scared. We found CD with the man. He had the man by the throat, and then I saw you, and CD started howling, and I couldn't reach Zack. Then they took you in the ambulance, and I couldn't decide if I should stay with CD or come to the hospital with you. Kelly said I should stay with CD, and then Zack called me back, and we came to the hospital, and, Jen, he ran the lights and siren, and oh, Jen, you are OK. We prayed you'd be OK."

Jen smiled, reached up to Paulie, and winced. She figured the shoulder was going to hurt for a while, given how much pain she felt now. Paulie reached down awkwardly and took her hand. Jen looked up, and her eyes locked on Zack. It felt like it was just the two of them. Paulie said something, and she pulled her gaze away. She assured Paulie she would be OK. He moved back, and Zack came and took her hand. He smiled reassuringly.

"What happened?"

"It was the brother of someone I had investigated and helped put in jail. He had been responsible for over twenty of our men being killed. After he went to prison, he apparently hung himself. His brother thought it was my fault. He came in to kill me, and CD lunged at him when he saw the gun. My sweet boy saved my life." CD's tail was wagging excitedly. He knew she was talking about him. "How did the operation go? Did you get them?"

Zack explained what he knew. He explained interrogations were going on all over the country. He told her the sheriff would be coming to take a statement and that her father was on his way. She thanked him. The nurse came in and told them she needed to give Jen a shot, and she needed to sleep. Jen encouraged Zack to go back to work, saying she was fine. He assured her he would be back. He turned to leave, took two steps, then turned around and quickly strode over to her. He leaned down and gave her an earth-shaking kiss. "We'll talk more later." Jen just nodded. She felt the effects of the shot and drifted back to sleep with a smile.

CHAPTER 57

Zack

For the next several hours, Zack was on the phone getting reports of the operation. Holly had been reunited with her parents.

He had talked with Cara and Jessica. Their stories were similar. They had been kidnapped and sold to an individual. They were sexually abused. They were made to work in the houses they lived in and were never able to leave the house. It appeared the offenders wanted younger girls, so they were being transported. Zack figured they were being sold so they could be prostituted. John had found their families. Cara's family was on their way to get her. The other girl's family had not been located yet.

They had a counselor standing by to talk with the girls and their families. The girls appeared to be fine physically, but there would be months of counseling before they could be fine mentally.

He had received reports from all the sites of the arrests, and the stories were similar.

Warrants had been served, and arrests made. One search warrant had revealed years of the trafficking and was a jackpot of where the victims were and who they had been sold to.

Zack was exhausted. He had been up for almost forty hours. Jacob had gone to the motel and gotten six hours of sleep. He had just walked in.

"You look like you've been dragged through a keyhole, backwards."

"Trust me, I feel like it." Zack filled him in on what had been happening and said he needed to go home and shower, then return to see Jen.

Jacob promised to call him if there was anything more he needed.

CHAPTER 58

Jen

Jen slowly opened her eyes and fought through the fog in her brain. She moved, felt the pain, and remembered she had been shot. She heard a rhythmic sound and realized it was snoring. Zack was there, with his head resting on the bed, sound asleep. She smiled.

At 7:00 a.m., the nurse came in to take her vitals. Zack stirred and looked at her and smiled. He smelled like cinnamon. He looked so tired.

"Have you been up all night and all day?"

Jen looked at him questioningly, and he nodded. They spent some time talking, and then Zack just sat by her bed while she slept. When she woke again, he said, "It is four in the afternoon. I sent Paulie and CD to your house with Kelly. Paulie insisted on staying because he told you he would. It took some convincing—that CD needed food and water. He was so tired he could hardly walk. Your father's flight should have landed thirty minutes ago."

Jen nodded and put out her hand. He took her hand and leaned down to kiss her on the cheek. She raised her eyebrows, and he smiled. "I think that is all I can handle right now. Jen, I was so scared I was going to lose you before I even told you I loved you. I realized it that day after I kissed you and then left. I wasn't sure you were ready to hear it." He went down on his knee and opened a small jewelry box. "I went out the next day and bought this ring. I wanted to do this in a much more romantic setting, but, well, Jen, will you marry me? I know we haven't known each—"

"Stop talking and kiss me. Yes, I will marry you." After a very satisfying kiss, she continued, "I realized I loved you the day Ingrid and Gordon met. When they talked about how comfortable they were with each other and how it just felt like they fit together, that's how I feel about you."

He leaned down and kissed her. This time, the kiss started out tenderly, and it appeared it might go on and on until Jen heard her father. "Well, I could come back if you tell me how long you need." Zack pulled back.

"Dad, you are here. I'm OK. Meet Zack, my … uh …"

"Yep, figured that out." He reached out and shook hands with Zack. "Good to meet you, Zack. Steve Standers. If I heard what I thought I just heard, congratulations. It takes a special man to win my Jen's heart. Thanks again for the phone call."

CHAPTER 59

Jen

Jen had been in the hospital for two days. She was to be released today. Her father got off the phone and sighed. Mary had fallen, and they were waiting to hear how she was. "She is going to have to have surgery."

"Dad, it's OK. Go. I have people here that will help, and she needs you."

About that time, a beautiful, white-haired woman swept into the room and went over and gave Jen a big hug. "I am Jessica, Zack's mom. I am here to meet my soon-to-be daughter-in-law and do whatever you need done to help."

Jen watched her father's surprised expression and then looked over to see Zack standing there, smiling.

Zack made the introductions. "Mom, this is Jen, and this is her father, Steve Standers. He just found out his wife fell and hurt herself, so we were trying to figure out what to do."

His mother was beaming. She walked over and shook Jen's

father's hand. "Well, it's decided. I brought my clothes, and I will go with Jen to her house and stay if she needs me or is willing to have me." She looked at Jen's father. "And you can rest assured I will take very good care of her." She turned and looked at Jen. "That is, if it is OK with you."

Jen smiled and nodded. Later, she told Zack, "I think I am going to like your mother very much."

Zack smiled and said, "She already likes you very much."

Jen's father regretfully took his leave and promised he would be back for the wedding.

Zack and his mother gathered Jen's things and walked beside the wheelchair as they took her to the car. His mother followed them in her car as they drove toward Jen's.

Paulie had been staying at Jen's with CD. Zack would take him home later. As he was helping her out of the car, the screen door flew open, and Paulie and CD came rushing toward her. Jen put up her hand. "Easy, guys."

Later as Jen and Zack's mother were sitting outside on the deck, enjoying the sunshine, Jen told her how thankful she was for how things had turned out. She shared with her how much Zack had talked about her and how much he loved her.

She smiled and said, "Well, I could say the same about you. I can see how much my son loves you and how happy you make him. Thank you."

Jen smiled and nodded. "He does love me, doesn't he?"

CHAPTER 60

Jake

Zack was tired. He had gotten a couple of nights of good sleep now that Jen was OK and his mother was taking care of her.

From files they had gotten with the search warrants, they had been making arrests all over the western states.

Zack dialed his brother. "Jake, we just found out about a place called the Shed. It is where boys were taken and taught to fight each other. Pretty bad stuff, Jake. We are planning to raid it today. It is an hour outside of Missoula, and I wonder if you would go with us. I figure these boys could be in pretty bad shape and will need some help."

Jake instantly agreed, and they scheduled a time to meet where he could accompany them. Jake suggested that he call in some favors and find some places for the boys to stay when they rescued them. They probably should not go back to their families, at least not at first. They would need some help adjusting.

As Jake hung up the phone, he put his head in his hand. "Lord, these boys are gonna need a lot of Your love. Help me show it to them. Help find safe places for them."

Then he went to work calling in favors from his contacts. He called his pastor and asked for the prayer chain to be activated. He couldn't give details yet, but they needed to be crying out to God.

CHAPTER 61

Trevor

Trevor lay on the thin mattress on the floor. He could not move and could barely breathe. He had lost the night before. He continued to hear the echoes of the crowd yelling for more and more blood. His opponent kept hitting and kicking. He knew he probably had broken bones, and he was having difficulty breathing. He knew he should get up and drink some water, but it hurt too much. Maybe this was it. He was going to die, right there in the cell. A life of worthlessness and a death by himself.

Vaguely he heard shouting but just allowed the tears to flow. Maybe death was welcome. At least there would be no more pain.

He realized the shouting was getting closer, and he heard feet running, and then the door to his cell was flung open. He heard what sounded like a hiss. Then he heard someone yell, "We need an ambulance."

Trevor felt the upper part of his body gently lifted into someone's lap. He passed out from the pain. When he came to, he heard someone talking gently.

"Father, this young man is so hurt and broken. He has been hurt too much. He has been so mistreated. Jesus, You know how that is. You know what it is like to be so tortured. I lift this young man up to You. I ask You to put Your hand on him and be with him and keep him alive. Help him to live so we might show him Your love instead of the evilness of those he has known."

Trevor felt a stinging on some of his wounds and realized the man holding him was crying and rocking him. As the tears fell on the wounds, the salt in them stung. No one had ever cried for Trevor. He did not remember anyone who had held him so gently.

More rushing feet, and then they were lifting him to the gurney. He passed out again from the pain.

Jake rode with him in the ambulance. Each time he came to, Jake assured him they would be at the hospital soon. He assured him that he was safe.

CHAPTER 62

Zack

Zack let himself into Jen's house. It had been a busy six months for Zack. Lots of arrests had been made. The trafficking ring had been shut down. Arrests had been made of those who bought the victims. There would always be someone out there to take their place, but for now, at least this group had been shut down.

Zack walked out to the patio, where he found Jen wrapped in a down blanket. She looked up and smiled as he came toward her. "Hello, wife-to-be."

"Hello, husband-to-be. How did the meeting go?"

He sat down next to her. "They offered me a promotion. I guess they felt like this was a big deal and wanted to promote me."

"That's great. What does that mean? Where will we go?" Jen swallowed the lump in her throat. She thought this might happen.

"If I take it, I will have to move to Seattle, at least for a while." He looked into her eyes and smiled. "I turned them down."

Jen gasped.

"I told them now was not a good time to leave. My heart is here, so I need to stay here. We need some time to get married and settle together as husband and wife."

"But this sounds like a big deal, and your career is important. Don't turn it down on my account. I don't want to hold you back."

"You are not holding me back. I love you, Jen. I like this area. I like what I do. I am not ready to sit in an office and push papers. I like being closer to my mom and Jake. Sometime down the road, if we both feel we are ready to move, well, then we'll consider it. Right now, you are stuck with me."

"Stuck sounds pretty good to me."

"I did some negotiating though, if you agree. I talked with them about keeping you on as a consultant for the entire Northwest. Our computer guys are overwhelmed, and it just makes sense to have someone around here to help us out. They agreed, if you will work under contract."

Jen nodded and smiled. "God is so good. I asked for guidance for where my life needed to go, and He filled it with you and a job. My life is so full; my cup overflows."

Zack mentioned Jake had called that morning before leaving Missoula. He told him that Trevor, the boy he had found at the Shed, was out of the hospital, and Jake had been able to get him moved into the group home he worked at.

"Jake has really been touched by this young man. I can tell he really cares about him and wants to help. He mentioned something about how this may change the direction of his life and work."

Jen nodded; how could this experience not change each of them?

Zack stood to go. "I need to go do a few things. Mom is at the apartment, and Jake will be arriving in an hour. Your dad and Mary are at the house they are renting for the week and should be over in an hour or so. Do you need anything?"

"I'm good. I am looking forward to tomorrow."

Zack swallowed the lump in his throat. "Me too."

CHAPTER 63

Jen and Zack

The ceremony had gone off without a snag. Jake had been Zack's best man, and Paulie had been Jen's, well, attendant. He had walked down the aisle with CD. The weather was cool but not arctic, which it could be in early March.

The ceremony had been in the church, and the reception at the local golf course. The decorations had been simple.

Jen sighed. She looked to where people were standing around talking and laughing. Her father and Mary were talking with Gordon and Ingrid. Mary had gotten her cast off just a few weeks ago and appeared to be completely recovered. Paulie and Kelly were standing in the corner. He said something, and she laughed. *Hmm, wonder what's happening there.* She had overheard them talking the day before. Paulie had insisted Tuesdays were days for chicken, and Wednesday for fish. Kelly had been telling him it was OK to change it. Zack's mother had come over a few minutes ago and hugged her. She gave really nice, tight hugs. Zack was talking with his brother and his girlfriend. He looked up, smiled, excused himself, and headed toward her. Jen was thankful for each person there.

Zack walked over, took Jen's hand, and pulled her toward the dance floor. It was a slow dance. Jen loved the feel of being in his arms; it felt safe. She looked up and saw the desire flare in his eye. Very softly, she said, "We have done the ceremony, we thanked the guests, we've cut the cake, I threw the bouquet. I think it would be OK to leave."

He smiled. "Mrs. Julion, I would like that very much."

They went to his mother and thanked her for her help. She assured her they would make sure the cleanup crew left everything in good shape. As she hugged Zack she whispered, "I am so proud of you, the man you are." Then she hugged Jen and whispered, "Thank you for making my son so happy. You are so special. I see why he loves you."

Her father came up and shook Zack's hand. "I know you will take good care of her," and then to Jen, "Be happy, my sweet girl."

Zack took Jen's hand, and they walked toward the car. Paulie and CD came running over. "I will take good care of CD while you are gone." Jen moved to hug him and saw him stiffen and then relax. "It's OK. You can hug me."

Together, Jen and Zack walked away, ready to begin their life as husband and wife.

RESOURCES

If you would like to know more about helping victims of human trafficking, here are some resources:

www.crossroadscares.org
https://polarisproject.org/
https://www.castl.org
www.dhs.gov.bluecampagn The Polaris Project
https://haltht.spcollege.edu/ Center for Human Trafficking Awareness
https://www.childwelfare.gov
https://www.themuse.com

If you suspect trafficking, report to National Human Trafficking Hotline, 888-373-7888, or text 233723.